The Devil's Dance

By the same author

Scandal's Daughter
Reasons of the Heart
The Quiet Rebel
The Choice

The Devil's Dance

JOANNA ERLE

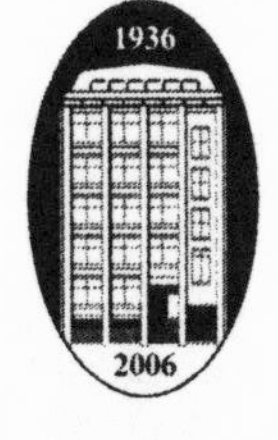

ROBERT HALE · LONDON

First published in Great Britain 2006

ISBN-10: 0-7090-8158-8
ISBN-13: 978-0-7090-8158-6

Robert Hale Limited
Clerkenwell House
Clerkenwell Green
London EC1R 0HT

2 4 6 8 10 9 7 5 3 1

Typeset in 11½/15pt Souvenir
by Derek Doyle & Associates, Shaw Heath
Printed in Great Britain by St Edmundsbury Press
Bury St Edmunds, Suffolk
Bound by Woolnough Bookbinding Limited

'To lead one the Devil's own dance.'
(To give one endless trouble: Brewer's Dictionary of Phrase and Fable)

CHAPTER ONE

'O Love's but a dance, where Time plays the fiddle!
See the couples advance. . . .'

Henry Austin Dobson

1846

TIMOTHY RYLAND OPENED the door into his parents' living-room upon an atmosphere of impending storm. He had expected to see only his father, but found Nicholas Mariott of Danesfield and his daughter, Rebecca, with him. The two men stood facing the door with the girl half hidden behind them, the spread of her blue crinoline skirts more visible than any other part of her.

A slight enquiring frown replaced the smile on the young man's face. Looking at his father, he said, 'You sent for me, sir?' and was startled by the flash of fury that crossed Joshua Ryland's face. Too late he remembered Josh preferred to be addressed as *Father* and not *sir*. Either of his brothers would have said *Pa*.

The slip was not enough to account for the threatening step Joshua took towards him, but before he could speak, Nick Mariott put a detaining hand on his arm, saying, 'No, Josh. Leave it to me.'

Timothy transferred his attentive gaze to the other man. There was anger in Nicholas Mariott's face, too; an anger as white and cold as his father's was hot and urgent for expression. Unmistakably, in both cases, the anger was directed at him. He could think of nothing he had done that could have caused it. For the past fifteen years there had existed between himself and Nick Mariott an affectionate uncle-and-nephew relationship though there was no blood link. It was an off-shoot of the deep-rooted friendship between Mariott and his father. Extending over forty years and crossing all boundaries between gentleman landowner and seaman, it was a friendship that surprised many who came late to Elswick and had not had time to grow used to it.

In a sharp-edged voice, Nick said to the youngest of his friend's three sons, 'Without any beating about the bush, Timothy, my daughter is four months into term with child and claims you are the father. Unmarried as she is, her situation needs speedy adjustment. Adjustment that should have been made well before this.'

There was silence in the room for some moments during which Timothy absorbed the several shocks that statement gave him. His training as a lawyer reminded him that he would be wise to keep emotion out of this as out of any other equation. He said evenly, 'It is the first I've heard of it.'

He stepped sideways to bring Rebecca's face into view. Barely five months past her seventeenth birthday, her eyes were reddened by weeping and her present expression was compounded of fear and misery. Even so, she was beautiful and her young face, under the braided, black silk coronet of her hair, held the promise of greater beauty to come. Her gaze was fixed on the floor. First names had been in use between them since childhood and questioningly, he said, 'Becca?'

The girl neither looked up nor spoke but the handkerchief she was twisting between her fingers shredded a little more.

More forcefully, Timothy said, 'Rebecca, look at me. Do you say I am the father?'

She sent one flaring, frightened glance towards him, nodded and returned her gaze to the floor, her lips soundlessly framing the word *yes*.

Timothy turned back to the two men. Face and voice carefully expressionless, to Nick he said, 'So what do you want from me?'

For a moment it looked as though Nick's icy control might break, but he mastered the threat and said thinly, 'Most certainly not insolence. Unhappily, I am in the position of having to ask you to put the matter as nearly right as can be done by marrying my daughter and as soon as it is possible.'

Again, Timothy turned to the girl. 'Is that what you want, Rebecca?'

She nodded, this time without even glancing up from her study of the floor.

'Very well.' Timothy's glance encompassed all three. 'It seems I have been called here only to add my agreement to the general one. You have it. So make what arrangements you please and I will comply with them.'

'Is that all you have to say?' Nick Mariott almost choked on the words.

Timothy's gaze locked with his. 'Yes, sir. That's all. It meets what you asked for, I think.'

He had advanced only a few steps into the room. Swinging round, he was gone in a moment, the door closing quietly on his exit.

Neither temperament nor training were proof against the rage that rose in him to smother all coherent thought as he started across the short distance from the house to the stable to collect the livery horse that would carry him back to his rooms in Chichester. Even so, he recognized the purposeful steps coming up behind him as his father's. When he looked round, Josh said to him, 'Go into the barn. I have a few words to say to you.'

Without answering, Timothy changed direction and went in through the open door of the small barn. Halfway into it, he stopped and turned about. In the same moment Josh came in, crashed-to the door and jammed a wedge into the latch.

The forcefulness of the action brought Timothy's mind back to full attention and pointed to the greater need for restraint on his own part. His father was not a man easily roused out of his normal attitude of slightly amused observation of the world around him. It was from him, Timothy knew, he inherited some part of his ability to look on a situation with a degree of detachment, a useful quality in a young man at the beginning of his career as a lawyer. He was aware now that, as in most cases, sound and fury would accomplish nothing. Even so, the tide of his own anger ran too high to allow him to do more than bring his green gaze up to meet the the vivid blue of his father's and say shortly, 'Well?'

A rush of blood darkened Josh's weather-browned face still more. 'Don't take that tone with me, boy. You're here for the thrashing you deserve and you're making it worse for yourself by the minute.'

For a moment Timothy stared at him in disbelieving astonishment before he snorted a mirthless laugh. 'Father! I'm twenty-four years old and no longer live at home.'

'I don't care what your age is, or where you live, I'm still your father and I'll see you get what you deserve. You disgust me! With all that you owe Nick Mariott you've brought his daughter down to ruin and disgrace and she little more than a child herself! You shamed yourself in doing it and me along with you. And adding to it now is your attitude – your damned indifference to it all. It's an insult to decency.' His voice was thick with a rage that was unusual in him and, as he spoke, he moved to shirt and flung it on top of his jacket.

Rarely as he gave way to rage, when given cause, it possessed Josh like a fever. The cool, analytical qualities of mind natural to him, fine-honed by experience, vanished; all thought narrowed down to focus on the object of his disgust. Just now it was centred in the young man before him and for all that only a short time ago he had claimed him as his son, it was almost without recognition of their relationship that he watched the lithe figure walk with catlike grace to the central post supporting the hay-loft. The easy movement was no different from what it was at any time, but seemed now to flaunt a lack of concern for what had been promised and to hint at the quiet insolence Nick had suspected in him earlier. To Josh at this moment it was an added provocation.

Reaching the post, Timothy turned to meet and hold his father's gaze, his own intense and searching. There was no visible easing in Josh's expression and what else he looked for, he did not find. With a grimace of distaste and an unmistakably contemptuous lift of his shoulders, he said, 'I am at your disposal, sir. Take what you want from me.' The green eyes glinted at his father with the same faintly malicious mockery that edged the words.

But goading Josh in his present mood was a risky game that brought swift punishment when the lash bit into his back while he was still turning and before he had taken hold of the post to steady himself. He staggered, shock ripping a ragged cry from him.

'That's the only note you'll crow on from now until I've finished with you, my young cockerel,' Josh told him grimly.

But having got a measure of what was to come, Timothy took a grip on the post and set himself to endure. No sound escaped him after that beginning except for the occasional rasp of a more deeply indrawn breath. How long it was before Josh threw the whip aside with an abrupt, 'Enough. I've done,' he could not have said. Long or short, the punishment had not been a light one: there was the taste of blood in his mouth from his bitten lips, and he knew he had been driven perilously close to the limit of his ability to endure in silence.

Josh watched him through narrowed eyes, his expression inscrutable. His anger vented, his mind was freed to register the darkening weals marring the pale gold of his son's back. He had never before flogged man or beast, though once a man had been flogged in his name by two men with reasons as good and better than he had. He had hit harder than he had realized and, he acknowledged to himself, not entirely in Rebecca Mariott's name. This, his youngest son, was the clever, educated one, not built to his own powerful pattern as the older two were, and not physically hardened by the gruelling toil of a seaman. For all that, the boy had shown man enough in the way he had borne what had been done to him. Head reared erect, he had stood rigidly still throughout, unyielding as the post that steadied him. The unexpected flash of approval pushed Josh into reminding himself that the thrashing had been merited: that so far the boy had not even hinted at an excuse, nor offered as much as the shadow of a regret for the mischief he had caused. At the same time he was conscious of a growing sense of unease; the suspicion that somewhere he had made a mistake; a wish that what had been done could be undone.

Still holding to the post, only now did Timothy allow his neck to bend sufficiently to permit his head to rest against the wood while he waited for the fiercest protests of his outraged flesh to subside and his legs to regain stability. Pride cut the time short, forced him upright and held him there. When he turned, there was no look about him of a man diminished by submission to humiliating punishment. The face he showed his father was that of a stranger, intolerant of eye, grim-mouthed and glitteringly hostile.

With steely clarity, he told Josh, 'The whip certainly added eloquence to your few words, sir. Now hear mine. First, my answer to the question neither you nor Nick Mariott asked me . . . I did *not* father Rebecca's child. Since the girl left her school, I have danced with her, danced attention on her. Nothing more. Becca is young, even for her age, and, as you know, her mother is still absent. Not surprisingly, she is frightened by her situation. I doubt she has the least idea of the effect fastening paternity on me can have. With half-a-dozen questions I could have got the truth from her.' He smiled grimly. 'I leave it to you to work out who would have been shamed then.'

He walked to where his shirt and jacket lay and, picking them up, turned to add, 'I shall not easily forget this day and not chiefly because of the flogging. What will live in my mind – what I shall not forgive – is the fact that *you* judged me guilty before ever I knew with what I was charged. *You* – without a flicker of doubt – accepted that I would serve Nick Mariott such an ill turn. Use Rebecca—' He broke off shaking his head in disgust. 'All you wanted from me was confession. My agreeing to marry the girl may have had that appearance, but what is *fact*, is that you had already judged and condemned me without a hearing.'

The smile he gave Josh now was like a dazzle of light on a newly sharpened blade. 'What I have told you is the truth. However, as a good lawyer should, I advise you to look to your own interest. In this context, that means disbelieving me and holding to what the girl said. You have just finished showing me how little difficulty you will have with that, so I will have no cause for fresh grief. Nor need you concern yourself that I shall go back on my agreement to give Rebecca Mariott's bastard my name. *Your* name, incidentally. It will cover whatever debt of kindness I owe her father. So let the wedding bells ring and much joy may we all have after.'

Careful to conceal any visible sign of wincing, he shrugged

his way into his shirt, not buttoning it but lapping one side over the other and tucking the ends into his waistband. Starting to put on his jacket, he thought better of it and hung it loosely on his shoulders. Almost casually, he said, 'I shall not willingly enter your house again, so you may send details of whatever arrangements you and Nick Mariott make to my rooms in Chichester and I'll honour them. I ask just one thing of you – no, *I demand it!* – and that is that you do not tell Nick anything of what has passed between us here in the barn, either spoken or done. That much you owe me.However her child was got, Becca has enough to bear. Let Nick keep his faith in what his daughter tells him. And on that I want your word.'

There was a pause before Josh jerked his head in unhappy token of agreement.

Across his shoulder, with another smile as razor-edged as the rest, Timothy said, as he walked past him, 'What you tell my mother to account for my absence is a problem you will need to resolve. In the unlikely event of her not extracting the truth from you, let me know what tale you settle on.'

Reaching the door, he pulled the wedge from the latch, dropped it on the ground and went out, leaving the door swinging.

CHAPTER TWO

TIMOTHY HAD LITTLE recollection of the journey back to Chichester; it was enough to be aware that, headed homeward, his hired horse ambled stolidly towards its stable. Arrived, he forced himself to concentrate and pay the liveryman his due. Walking the short distance to his rooms afterwards, his unsteady steps compelled recognition of how much strength had been leached from his body by the beating he had taken.

He had some vague memory of pulling off his boots in his bedroom and throwing himself face down on the bed. There he lay through the night, his back aflame and too painful to allow him to sleep except for brief periods during which he slipped into an exhausted doze. The night seemed unnaturally long. When at last he heard his landlord moving about the house, he heaved himself off the bed and, standing in the doorway, called until he caught the old man's attention. Unable to face forcing his inflamed skin to bear the weight and rub of clothes, with a suitable bribe, he persuaded the landlord to send the grandson who ran his errands with a message to his partners, Diment and Frewen, informing them he was too unwell to come to the office today but expected to be there tomorrow.

It was early on Wednesday morning when a knock at the door of his small office, brought Timothy's head up from the papers he was studying. The door opened and one of the young clerks from the general office, half in and half out of the room, said, 'Lady to see you, sir. Says she's your mother. Urgent she says.'

'Right. Show her up, will you, Pete.'

He stood up and came round the desk and two minutes later Prue Ryland came in. She was an active woman and her figure was very little plumper than it had been in youth, but laying a hand on her unstressed bosom, she said in mock protest, 'My, your stairs are steep.'

He did not advance towards her, but stood waiting in unsmiling silence.

Prue frowned. 'No greeting, Timothy?'

'Until I know whether an embrace would be welcome, Mother, no.'

She gave an exasperated shake of her head. 'Great heavens! You men! No matter what has happened nothing alters the fact that you're my son. Do I have to ask for your kiss?'

His expression softened; he moved towards her, put his arms round her and kissed her smooth cheek.

With a fierceness that was half annoyance, she hugged him in return. He flinched and she drew back to look at him, 'As bad as that?' she asked.

'Bad enough.' He shrugged it aside and turned to pull a chair forward for her, then returned to his own. Green gaze met green across the desk. He smiled fleetingly, bleakly. 'So he told you?'

'Yes, of course.'

'Of course, indeed.' Another small, bitter smile flickered and died.

'He was more reluctant to tell me than I have ever known him to be. What happened between you sits uneasily with him. But what I don't understand is why it was not until after he had taken the whip to you that you claimed the child was not yours.'

'He had already decided my guilt and was in no mood to

listen to anything I said. Had I tried earlier, he would have thought I was making a shabby attempt to escape punishment. Later, it had the virtue of sharpening the point that he had made up his mind without as much as pausing to question whether or not the charge was true.' His eyes gleamed a challenge at her. 'Do *you* think I seduced Rebecca Mariott? Or are they calling it rape now?'

'I know you well enough to be certain that whatever it was, you had nothing to do with it. Little Becca – *no*, you would not!' Her belief was absolute. 'And even if you had, I'd still be your mother – though not a proud one, I grant you.' Her brief slanting smile mirrored his.

'Thank you.' He passed a hand swiftly over his face as though to wipe any reflection of the importance of her answer out of his expression. 'There is no way to prove my claim except through Becca and I won't do that to the poor child. But it's a pity my father knows me so little he has no share of your faith in me.'

'*Josh*. . . .' Prue shook her head ruefully. 'Have mercy on him, Timothy. As a seaman he has made few mistakes in his lifetime and as a man it's been the same. If in the end he has to accept he made one over this, it will go hard with him because of what he did.'

'Will it!' The tone was sardonic. 'Well, I'm likely to carry some of the scars of his mistake on my back for the rest of my life. My memory of how I came by them is likely to last equally long.'

Prue was quick in her husband's defence. 'The beating you took was the price you paid for pride. Even if Josh did not question you directly, the question was there. What did you expect him to think when Rebecca was claiming you for the father and you were agreeing to marry her? Come to that, why did you?'

There was long pause before Timothy said, 'Several reasons

contributed to it. You will have to forgive me if I do not enumerate them.'

'I'm quite good at guessing where my sons are concerned.'

'Then I have no need to answer your question.' He gave her a shadowy smile.

'Try for some understanding,Timothy. To Josh, Rebecca is the daughter we don't have. He was angry and over full with loathing for what he thought you had done.'

'The point, Mother, is that he so readily thought it. Without one question directed to me! *That* gave me the measure of the value he sets on me. But then, I'm not a seaman and I'm not made in *his* image as are Andy and Giles. I'm superfluous to his needs and offending him, too, I imagine, by resembling you, but not actually being female.'

Prue rounded on him. 'That, Timothy Ryland, is a wicked thing to say! Josh values you no less than he values Andy and Giles. Nor does he think you any less of a man because you don't look like him.'

He met her indignant glare unmoved. 'After Sunday's showing you'll find me hard to convince.'

'Then listen carefully to what I say now. Josh went against his own nature when he brought you back here from France and handed you over to another man's care. For *your* benefit, not his. Andy and Giles worked for their father aboard the lugger from the age of twelve. Full time from the age of fifteen. That they chose to, I'll allow. But it doesn't change the fact that at that age you were living the life of a gentleman's son at a school for gentlemen's sons and then at university. It wasn't Nicholas Mariott who paid for it, it was Josh. All of it. And any extra you needed or wanted, including buying into this law-firm partnership afterwards. If anyone has the the right to complain, it's your brothers.'

Timothy held up a hand. 'I dispute none of it. For what my father did for me in the past, for what he gave me, I honour him and I'm grateful. Though I'll remind you, Mama, that unlike Andy and Giles, I was not offered a choice about any of it except the partnership – and for that he'll be repaid at the earliest it is in my power!' His expression hardened and his lips thinned. 'On Sunday he *did* give me a choice. One that treated me as less than a man. Under threat of his superior strength, my father allowed me to decide between meekly submitting to a whipping, or being forcibly tied to a post to be whipped like an unmanageable cur.'

He stared unseeing across the desk, the silence heavy and painful until he said, flatly, 'Once, there was no man on earth I admired more, but *that* choice altered both how I see him and how I feel towards him.'

It had altered a great deal more, Prue recognized, and shook her head in despair this time. She could guess the depth of offence given to her son in the pride of his young manhood to be forced, as he had been, to accept a thrashing. But that was not the crux of the matter: it was what there was beyond that counted most with this, their youngest son. The pity was that he was the one who would be the first to discern and the last to forgive a failure of trust. Her heart ached for him, but the steel she had often suspected to be present in a seemingly easy-going young man was clearly visible to her now. It was Josh for whom she grieved: Josh, who through the years, had loved and protected them all with a fierceness that would not have stopped short of murder had actual harm threatened any one of them: as Nick Mariott had recognized long ago when Andy had been so threatened. It had been a testimony to the strength of the friendship between the two men that Nick, without hesitation, to save Josh from the consequences he would have so recklessly drawn down on himself, had incapacitated him by shooting him.

'Between the two of you—' she began, but broke off abuptly to say, 'But Timothy, all that must wait. I have yet to tell you why I'm here . . . why I was not here yesterday or the day before. It has to do with Rebecca. She's lost the baby and is barely alive herself.'

Timothy sat very still. 'Go on,' he said.

'It happened on Monday . . . late in the afternoon. . . . At the time her mother arrived home from France. An accident. Rushing to meet her, we think, she fell down those awkward stone steps in the Danesfield garden and it's supposed she wasn't found for some long while. It took time for the doctor to be fetched and no one at Danesfield knew how to stop the bleeding before he came.' Tears came into her eyes. 'She's so weak! Doctor Bartlett doesn't hold out much hope. She's lying in a kind of stupor, but from time to time she says your name. Not calling you exactly . . . just saying it as though you lie heavy on her mind. What a homecoming for poor Elise! She asks if you'll go to Danesfield. She thinks your presence might comfort Rebecca if she could be made aware of it.'

Long moments passed before Timothy said, 'Was there ever such a damnable tangle!' He sighed. 'I'll come, of course, but what good my presence will do—' He left it unfinished, locked away the papers he had been studying, then looked up sharply at her. 'There's just one thing: has my father told Nick Mariott any part of what went on between us in the barn?'

'No. None of it. He gave you his word, didn't he?'

'If one considers the ease with which he reached his judgement of me, I'm entitled to one doubt of him,' He saw her expression change and said hurriedly, 'No, no. Take no notice of me. I don't mean to add to your cares. I imagine you came in the gig? I'll see you on your way, then get a horse from the livery stables and follow.'

She stood up. 'If you go by the bridleways you'll still arrive before me. Wait for me at home.'

'No.' His expression turned bleak. 'I told my father I would not willingly go to his house again and I meant it. I'll meet you at the entrance to Danesfield.'

There was a note in his voice that warned her not to argue and she turned and went with him down the stairs. He saw her into the gig, then stepped back into the front office to say where he was going before setting off for the livery stables in the next street.

There was no point in pushing the horse over the shorter distance and he came to Danesfield's gates only a short time before the gig arrived. At the house, a groom and a stableboy appeared to attend to the horses and Prue led the way into the hall. Nick and Elise Mariott were standing talking at the far end. The moment his gaze fell on Timothy, Nick's expression darkened. He acknowledged Prue briefly but with courtesy, then swung away and went through into his bookroom study.

At forty, Elise Mariott was still a handsome woman, though looking tired and drawn just now. She came to meet mother and son and to say to Timothy in a husky voice drained of all emotion, 'Thank you for coming. We'll go up at once, if you please. We don't know how much t-time—' she stumbled over the word, made an effort and finished, 'time there is. And the doctor is expected to return shortly, too.'

The room they entered was a young girl's room, the colours pale and pretty, with delicate muslin curtains at the windows and falling from a crown above the bed-head. There was a faint sweet scent on the air that he recognized at once as one he associated with Becca. Leading Timothy to one side of the bed, Elise went to stand at the other.

Except for the occasional, slight to-and-fro movement of her head, Rebecca lay white and still, looking almost transparently fragile, her long black hair flaring across the pillow. As he watched, Timothy saw his name take shape on her bloodless lips. If ever she had made the word audible, it was so no longer.

He reached for one of the slender hands lying slackly on the bedcovers and then looked at Elise for permission. She nodded.

Sitting down in the chair drawn close to the bed, he bent towards the girl and said softly, 'Becca, it's Timothy. I'm here.'

Nothing indicated that she heard him. He repeated the same words several times with equal lack of result. The weak, intermittent movement of her head continued. Suddenly, in a strong, authoritative voice, Timothy said, 'Becca, listen to me. There's nothing for you to worry about. *Nothing*! I understood.'

The veined eyelids fluttered, opened sufficiently to show a gleam of the eyes beneath and instantly closed again. The fingers of the cold, limp hand he held twitched in the smallest of movements and very faintly she sighed. Then all movement stopped. Timothy lifted his shocked gaze to Elise who put out a fearful hand to seek the pulse in the girl's other wrist. Struggling against tears, she shook her head and said, 'She has slipped back into coma. The doctor said she might do so.' And then, almost to herself, added, 'Said, too, she might not wake from it.'

As though on cue, there was a quiet knock at the door. A maid entered to say in a hushed voice, 'Doctor Bartlett, ma'am,' and stood aside to allow the doctor to enter.

Prue touched her son's arm. 'There's no more to be done now. Come. We'll go.'

At the bottom of the stairs Nick Mariott stood waiting. To Timothy, he said, 'I will see your mother into her gig. I want a word with you, if you will be good enough to wait for me here.' Face and tone were bleakly expressionless, his dark eyes as black and hard as flint.

Timothy waited. Returning, Mariott pushed to the door behind him and stood before it. He remained silent for several long moments studying the younger man he had believed he knew so well, looking for change that would match the change of character that had surely taken place. None was visible. As always, he was a good-looking youngster with a clean, sharp beauty of bone under fine-textured skin lightly tanned by coastal sunlight and sea breezes. It looked the face of an honest being, not that of one who who would betray trust. Nick swallowed a cynical laugh at his own gullibility.

Quietly, but with a pulse of violence beating through the words, he said, 'I have just two things to say to you, but I had no wish to upset your mother by saying them in front of her. The first is, that if by some miracle my daughter survives, there will be no marriage between you. There is no longer the need, and I now think her death preferable to seeing her married to the man you have become. For the rest, you will never approach her again in any way and after today you will never again enter this house. If Rebecca *does* die, take care not to cross my path, because if you do, I cannot answer for what I may do. Have I made myself clear?'

'Yes, sir.'

Nick waited as if expecting more, staring at him as though pushed to the limit of wonder when nothing came. Words finally exploded from him. 'We trusted you, damn you! Do you have nothing to say to that? Not one extenuating circumstance to offer? No apology? *Nothing*?'

In the circumstances as they appeared to Nick Mariott, he was entitled to his anger, Timothy thought. He felt no resentment towards him and hid his compassion for the man. A very different matter from how he felt towards his own father. He wished he might offer sympathy, but was certain that to do so in the circumstances in which they were snarled would appear to Nick as the grossest insult.

Speaking carefully, keeping all inflection from his words, he said, 'As Rebecca's situation was, and as matters now stand, I can think of nothing that can be said in extenuation. Nor can I think of anything other I can say that you can want to hear. Except perhaps this: if Rebecca dies, the chance is that my father will despatch me to follow her before ever you reach me.' A small bleak smile turned his lips for a moment. 'Between you, Becca will not go unavenged, I think. It may not seem sufficient – may not satisfy you – but it is all I have to offer.' He paused as though to allow Nick to respond to that and when he did not, went on, 'If there is nothing else, sir, will you excuse me. I wish to speak to my mother before she drives home.'

The quiet level at which the words were spoken, with nothing in them of bravado or self-pity, took from them any hint of melodrama. The tone echoed queerly in Nick's mind: it seemed to hold a kind of desolate dignity, as though this boy he had seen grow to manhood had already come to terms with the possible consequences of Becca's death and even accepted them. It left Nick baffled. Without another word, he stood away from the door to watch the man who had brought so much misery to his house pass out from it.

With Timothy on his mind, he walked slowly through the hall towards his study, his earlier intention to follow the doctor up to Rebecca's room forgotten. For a time, he had seen more of the boy than of any of the Rylands, even Josh himself. In the last years of the Admiralty blockade of the coasts of Kent and Sussex by which it was hoped to bring to an end the rampant smuggling in which the two counties were then engaged, Josh, finding his family under threat from an over-zealous naval officer, had taken them all to live in France. On a dark night – the usual prerequisite when Josh visited his homeland at that time and five years after the self-imposed exile had begun – he had brought 10-year-old Timothy to Danesfield for Nick to arrange the higher education his French teachers said his intelligence deserved. That for Josh, a temporary Frenchman only, meant an English education.

Until now, Nick had never regretted using his influence to get the boy accepted, first at Winchester, his own old school, and later at Balliol, his sometime college at Oxford. Holidays were generally spent here at Danesfield until the end of the blockade and the return of the other four members of the family. The young Timothy, Nick remembered, was self-contained, with something of quicksilver in both mind and movement and a chameleon ability to adapt to his environment. He took on the polish offered by public school and university as easily as he absorbed knowledge and without losing any part of his individuality. He shared something of Josh's quizzical attitude to the world around him, but Timothy's amusement was more private and less noticeable than his father's. Even after the rest of the Ryland family returned to England, the boy had still run tame at Danesfield.

On a surge of indignation, Nick pushed back the invading and misplaced sympathy: it was Timothy Ryland who had brought his daughter to ruin and cast the black shadow of her likely death upon himself and his wife.

Once, Nick thought, I may have known him. But that Timothy had been a boy; he was dealing now with the man he had become. How much did he know of the changes that had taken place in the transition from one state to the other? How could he know what potential for good or ill had lain dormant in the boy's blood until the time came for them to grow to power?

CHAPTER THREE

ELISE MARIOTT ACCOMPANIED the doctor to the door of the house when he left, then walked into her husband's study to find Nick sitting in black and cheerless contemplation of something far distant.

'You did not come up when the doctor came,' she said.

He looked at her, focusing slowly as though waking from a dream. Or a nightmare. 'No,' he said. 'I wanted a word with young Ryland. Afterwards I—' He shook his head, left the sentence unfinished and standing up, came to wrap her in his arms, holding her close. 'Is there any change?'

She nodded against his shoulder and he held her a little way off to look in her face. Saw the tears brim and spill and said, 'Oh my poor darling. And I not there!' He pulled her close again. 'I'm sorry . . . sorry.'

She pushed back to look up at him. With a valiant attempt at a smile, she said, 'Nick, it's better not worse. A little more hope. She hasn't lapsed into coma, as I thought . . . she's fallen asleep. Doctor Bartlett says it is the best thing that could happen. He thinks she may sleep for a long time and have gathered some strength when she wakens. We must not be *too* optimistic, he said, but we need not altogether despair.'

'Thank God! Even so small a relief as that is something.' He made a sound of disgust in his throat. 'What is it about Josh's sons? The eldest stabs me when he's only fifteen and comes close to killing me and twenty years later, the youngest brings my daughter to ruin and perhaps death.'

'Nick, it was Timothy who gave Becca the peace she was needing and perhaps a chance to live,' Elise said gently. 'He sat beside her holding her hand, saying, *I'm here*, but she did not seem to hear or notice, though he said it a number of times. But suddenly loudly, almost fiercely, he said, *Listen to me. There's nothing to worry about. I understood.* At once Becca's eyes half opened, she gave a little sigh and sank down into sleep. It was as though she had been hanging from a rope in the dark, afraid to let go because she could not see the ground, but Timothy's words reassured her and she let go to find the ground only inches under her feet.'

'Are you now asking me to be grateful to him for that when he is the root cause of our daughter's ruin and our distress? I can tell you I'm not!' Nick's bitterness rang like iron on iron. 'From beginning to end, he has not said a word about abusing our trust, or ruining our daughter's life. When he agreed to marry her it was as though he were conferring a favour on us all. If he had shown some regret – claimed he was drunk at the time – was madly in love with her and carried away— But no, nothing! He responds to everything I say with the same quiet civility which for some reason only angers me the more. At times I don't know how I have kept from striking him.' He turned from her to stare again into some far unquiet distance. When he turned back, he said, 'Don't look to him for further miracles, Elise, because a short time ago I told him he would never set foot in this house again. I told him too, that if Becca dies, I could not answer for what my actions might be. And I meant it!'

'Oh, Nick! So much unhappiness . . . so much spoiled. How is it all to end?'

'It disturbs *you*! But does it disturb young Timothy? Not a bit!

Had anyone ever said he would turn out like this I would not have believed them. I no longer understand him. As civil as ever, he told me that though it might not be enough to satisfy me, his father would probably be before me in killing him if Becca dies. And he spoke as though he cared as little about that as about the rest.'

Elise took his hand and drew him to sit beside her on a sofa. Laying a hand on his knee, she said, 'Would Timothy's attitude seem so strange if he were *not* the father of the child Becca has conceived?'

'You are not going to tell me you think Becca lied? I don't believe it! Why should she? Who else has there been? Whenever he has been free, the boy has been her shadow the whole summer through. Only *he* has had so much opportunity. *No*! Why should she lie?' He was on his feet again. 'And why should he accept the charge? Carry the blame? Agree to marry her? Take on responsibility for another man's by-blow?'

'It was just a thought . . . that if he loves Becca, he might.'

'A perfect knight! Sir Galahad come again? It's too much to expect of any man! No, Elise! What I believe is that the boy is clever to the point of cunning. A short time ago he first reduced me to a state of impotent rage, then brought me to a ridiculous feeling of compassion for him; of feeling the loneliness of his position with Josh almost as angry with him as I am. A little more thought, however, made me wonder if my intelligence had not been been subtly insulted and I unable to see it. After all, Elise, it would be no disadvantage to him to marry our daughter, would it? He's clever enough to have taken that into consideration. And he's as slippery as an eel. He side-steps questions and everything he says seems to be a little aslant. It's as if we merely *seem* to speak the same language because we make the same sounds, but the words themselves have quite different meanings. I tell you, young as he is, he's too subtle for me.'

Elise sighed unhappily. 'Whatever the truth, at present

nothing matters to me except Rebecca. And Nick—' She waited for his full attention. 'If that involves begging Timothy to come again to the house you have banned him from, I shall do it. When you are safely elsewhere, of course.'

He reached for her hand and held it tightly in his. 'You may beg the Devil himself to visit if it will help our girl, my darling. I promise to be blind and deaf and dumb.'

Rebecca slept for ten hours after Timothy's visit and then, slowly, slowly, began to find a little strength. It was more than two weeks before she was able to sit out of bed for a time each day, friends were allowed to visit for short periods on the strict understanding they did not excite her or overtax her in any way. Her illness was explained as a bad fall, internal injuries and being too long unconscious before she was found. If there was speculation, nothing was actually known and either Elise or Rebecca's old nurse, Nannibet, was always at hand to ward off danger when questions approached treacherous ground.

Then came days when she was carried downstairs by Nick to sit for an hour or two beside the fire in the small parlour that was kept mainly for Elise's use, with Elise or Nannibet to sit with her, busy with their sewing. Rebecca herself was unable yet to apply herself even to a task making so small a call on her energies as embroidery. On the third occasion she was brought down her hands lay idly on the shawl that had been placed over her legs, but after a time began nervous play with the fringe. Silence lay between them for some time and then Rebecca said quietly, 'Timothy hasn't come to see me.'

Elise allowed herself a cautious glance at her daughter but found no guidance in the the girl's expression. As carefully expressionless, she said, No.'

'Are we not now going to be married?'

'No. It is no longer necessary. I thought you understood that.'

'Oh.' Rebecca lapsed into silence for a short time, then,

faintly wistful, asked, 'Doesn't he want to?'

Elise allowed her gaze to meet her daughter's this time and said, 'Surely you can answer that question better than I can?'

'I – I thought perhaps he might.' Rebecca looked away.

Elise let her sewing rest in her lap, drew breath and trying to keep any suggestion of emotion out of her tone, said, 'That sounds oddly cool to me in view of what must have happened between you. If he had no real feeling for you, surely your feelings for him must have been very strong to allow it. Or did he force you?'

Rebecca looked shocked. 'No! Oh, no! He wouldn't.'

'So how did it happen?'

Rebecca stared at her as if the question had been spoken in a language of which she knew nothing. 'I – it— *Oh, Mama!*' She burst into tears.

Elise went to kneel beside her and clasp her in her arms, not probing further for fear of setting back this dearly loved child's recovery. After a time, as the first fierceness of the paroxysm began to abate, Rebecca mumbled into the tear-sodden stuff of her mother's gown, 'It wasn't Timothy: it was Edward Jordan.'

Between sobs and snuffles, the story was told. Her come-out party in May, her first glass of champagne, the flattering attention of a good-looking man of thirty, a foolish but innocently undertaken walk with him through the starlit gardens to the gazebo where he had produced glasses and more champagne from his pockets.

'I think he filled my glass whenever I wasn't looking. And then . . . and then I did not seem to know what was happening. I felt dizzy and strange. And what he did hurt me. Afterwards he said it was something adults did for pleasure but did not talk about. I would find out all about it in time, but meanwhile forget it. But as time went by and – things did not happen, Nannibet started asking questions and by then, *you* were away in France with the Chevenens and I did not know what to do. When your return was delayed the second time, Nannibet said too much time was passing and Papa had to be told. And Papa was so angry and so cold, demanding to know who was the man, saying whoever he was he would have to marry me. I knew Edward Jordan was already married and miles away in London and I was frightened, so I said it was Timothy because he had always been my friend . . . always helped me and I thought he would understand and wouldn't mind marrying me.'

'*Oh, Becca*!' Elise closed her eyes in horror at her daughter's naïvety and this further complication of the situation. She said unhappily, 'How am I to tell your papa this!'

'Oh, no, Mama! Please, *no*! Does he need to be told? I can't bear it! He is so— Since I've lost the baby and Timothy has said he'll marry me. . . .' Her voice tailed off as she saw her mother's face.

'Because there is no baby, you are not forced into marriage. Don't you realize how angry your father is with Timothy? He has told him he will not be marrying you . . . will not be allowed to come here any more. You seem not to have any idea what you have done to him, Becca. He is in deeper disgrace than you, condemned and reviled by your father and his own. He no longer visits his home even. He has taken all the blame, supported you loyally throughout, never saying a word in his own defence! Agreed without quibble to marry you. You owe him a very great deal.' She looked at her daughter with sad compassion. 'I'm sorry, my dear, your father *must* be told. He is angry *for* you rather than *with* you. Apart from anything else, we owe it toTimothy that he is cleared of blame.'

Rebecca's tears were wild and bitter by this time and Elise was forced to turn her attention to soothing her into a quieter state. She rang then for Nannibet to take the girl back to bed and give her a composer. Mr Mariott not being available, she was carried upstairs by James, once footman, but now a stolid man of forty-six and promoted to the dignity of butler and of being Mr Sharman to the lesser staff.

Thankful Nick was out on some business of the estate, Elise went by the shore path which passed through Danesfield land to Blackthorns, the Rylands' large cottage which long ago had been built close to the sea on an acre of ground sold to Josh's father by Nick's father. As she expected, she found Prue Ryland alone in the house except for a girl working in the kitchen, so there was no bar to the private conversation she wanted with the older woman.

When it ended, it was difficult to say which of the two women was in deeper apprehension of the reaction of her husband to the information they had exchanged.

Elise chose the quiet half-hour before their seven o'clock dinner in which to tell Nick what Rebecca had told her. Seeing his face darken, she hurried into excuses for their daughter . . . her youth, inexperience, lack of knowledge, her helplessness against the duplicity of a ruthless man of the world intent on despoiling her. And finally her panic at finding herself in a seemingly hopeless situation and her mother away from home.

Having listened in silence, Nick remained so for some long moments when she finished, staring at her unseeing. When he spoke at last, it was to say, '*Timothy*! When I think of the contempt I poured on the boy!' And then almost angrily, 'Why should he allow it? Accept blame for what he did not do? *Why*?' Restlessly, he got to his feet, strode away a short distance, turned and came back to where Elise sat. 'You thought it possible he might be in love with the girl. Perhaps you were right. *Do* you think that is the reason?'

'I don't know. He has been fond of her from the very beginning when Josh first left him with us, unlikely as it seemed when she was a mere tot of three and he a ten-year-old schoolboy. But Nick, there's something else you ought to know. I went to see Prue and told her what Becca had said. I thought it better she should break it to Josh than you should. She told me something in return. Something none of us here at Danesfield has known. Something that even now Becca must not hear about. She isn't yet strong enough to bear the responsibility.'

She paused and he snapped, 'Well?'

'That Sunday . . . when Timothy walked out of the Rylands' living-room, Prue says Josh followed him.'

Nick nodded. 'Yes, I seem to remember he did.'

'Josh told Timothy to go into the barn attached to their stables and having got him there, thrashed him with a whip. Under threat from Josh to tie him to a post, knowing he could not match his father's strength and reluctant to raise his hand against him in any case, Timothy offered no resistance. It was a severe beating, Prue says, but he stood and suffered it without a murmur. Only when it was over, he pointed out to Josh that neither he nor you had asked him to confirm what Rebecca said. He told him, too, that he was *not* the father of our daughter's child. Then he made Josh swear not to tell *you* that, or anything else that had happened from the time they had entered the barn. And to confuse everything thoroughly, he advised Josh for his own sake not to believe what he, Timothy, had just told him, but to stand by what Becca had claimed. Last of all he said he would not willingly enter his father's house again.'

'Dear God! Is there no end to the nightmare! What am I to say to either of them?'

Looking at him, Elise said sadly, 'What is Josh to say to his son?'

At ten the following morning, Nick, never one to shirk responsibility, entered a small room on the first floor in the pleasant old building in Chichester that housed the highly reputable firm of lawyers, Dimont and Frewen. Though it could not be called drear, the room gave an impression of being quietly grey and barely furnished, yet seemed to contain all that was necessary to its purpose. The smell of old, leather-bound books crossed with the metallic odour of freshly made ink, seemed to contribute to the austere character of it all, which was, Nick supposed, to be thought suited to the status of a junior partner on probation in a long-established and respected firm of lawyers. Timothy met him with grave courtesy, set a chair for him, walked back to his own and waited until Nick was seated before seating himself Across the desk, he watched the older man with wary composure, braced for attack, but with no clue as to what shape it might take.

Nick came straight to the point. 'What I have to say is not easily said but it is honestly meant. I am here to apologize, humbly, on my own behalf and on that of my daughter. Yesterday, Rebecca confessed she lied in naming you the man responsible for her pregnancy. On her behalf I can plead youth, ignorance, panic at her situation and her mother's absence. She named you as the friend who would help her in her need and without the least understanding of the possible consequences to you . . . the several ways in which her lie would affect you. For myself I can offer no excuse. I condemned you on too easy an acceptance of misinformation.'

It took Timothy a little time to adjust to the suddenness of this reversal, though he allowed nothing of what he felt to show in his face. Only when he was sure he had equal control of his voice, did he say, 'I do not see that you need an excuse for accepting what your daughter told you, Mr Mariott. It must have appeared to you that I confirmed what Rebecca said when, without protest, I agreed to marry her.' Hurriedly, he headed off any comment Nick might have made about that by asking, 'Do you now know who was the man responsible?'

'Edward Jordan. At her coming-out party. He plied her with champagne to which she was totally unused and having got her alone and more than halfway drunk, raped her. She was too unknowing of what was happening for it to be called seduction.'

Timothy had dropped his gaze to the desk top. He gave Nick one quick glance and looking down again said quietly, 'I thought it might be Jordan. A man of the world with an eye for the prettier girls. Also a stranger to Elswick, married and living in London.'

'And only at the party because he was staying with the Colbrookes at the time. A nephew, or great-nephew, I believe. What can I do about him without distressing the Colbrookes, so long our friends and now so very elderly?' He let a moment or two pass while he fought his frustration before saying, 'But that must wait. What I want to say to you, Timothy, is to ask if you can bring yourself to regard the harsh things I have said to you recently, as unsaid? And believe me more than grateful for what you were willing to do for Rebecca? No light thing for any man to do.'

'Of course.'

'As easily as that? You're very forgiving.'

'It depends, I think, on circumstances and the nature of the offence. And, of course, the offender.'

Nick regarded him sombrely. Said slowly, 'Which, I think, brings us to your father. . . . Becca doesn't know what happened between you and Josh in the barn. I don't think she could ever forgive herself if she did.'

Light flared briefly behind the level green gaze. 'I should prefer her not to know. Now or at any time. I am a little surprised that you do.'

'Your mother and my wife were the means. I understand you did not exempt your mother from knowing.'

Something close to a smile touched Timothy's face for an instant but did not settle. 'No. I knew I could not. I thought my father would impress on her my . . . my request for you not to be told. It did not occur to me she would tell Mrs Mariott.'

'It was only after my wife had told your mother what Rebecca had confessed.' He paused to draw deep breath having arrived at the crucial point. 'Timothy, what happened between you and Josh is one of the worst aspects of the whole unhappy matter. I regret it with all my heart. If there was anything I could do to make amends for it, I would. Do not, I beg you, let it make a permament rift between you and Josh.'

Timothy's gaze removed from his face to some distant point beyond him. 'I cannot separate the offender from the offence. What may be regarded as mere misjudgement in one can be unforgivable in another.'

'If you can forgive Becca and myself, you must forgive Josh!'

Swift and bright as summer lightning, the green gaze re-engaged with his. 'I am sorry to disagree with you. Rightly or wrongly, what happened between my father and myself is beyond my capacity to forgive. But you have no need to concern yourself. I have drawn a line under it. There will be no further consequences.'

Nick stared at him, shaking his head. After a moment or two, he said, 'Be careful, Timothy. That is something of which you cannot be certain. Consequences have a way of waiting like sharks beneath the ocean's surface. Do you think that when Josh learns what you now know, he will not come to see you?'

'I hope he will not. I should be sorry to deny him admittance.'

That shook Nick. 'You would not! No! You *could not* do it!'

Timothy's brows rose briefly in a surprise Nick was certain was unfeigned. 'Again I must disagree with you. It would save us both greater embarrassment.'

Did he think words would keep Josh out if he chose to come in? But that apart, there was something in the certainty with which Timothy spoke that made Nick pause. The contrast with the generosity he himself had received was disturbing. This, he thought, was a Timothy he had not seen before. Nothing he could say was going to make any impression on a mind so utterly resolved against remitting any part of its grievance against his father. A valid grievance, and yet—

Following a lengthy silence, he changed tack and said, 'It was uncommonly generous of you to support Becca's lie . . . why did you?'

Timothy took time to answer as though the question needed consideration. A little wryly, he said finally, 'I think my foremost reason was that I saw myself as the friend in need that she thought me.'

Nick did not doubt the truth of that, but wondered if it were all the truth. He said slowly, 'That is to put a high price on friendship.'

'Not as high as you have put it in the past when Andy nearly killed you.'

'You know about that?'

'Brothers talk. When there are three, the youngest often has – needs – the longest ears.'

'It was a long time ago . . . all of twenty years. He was fifteen. He did not intend to kill me. Trapped in the dark of the stable between me and my horse, he was frightened. Anxious to escape, he just struck out.'

'So Andy said. He was more afraid of your ill-tempered Turkoman than the worsening odds with your grooms approaching the stable door.' Now, momentarily, he allowed himself a fine-edged smile.

They lapsed into silence as though an end had been reached. He had come in hope of absolution, Nick thought, and it had been given him more readily and with greater grace than he had any right to expect. The more surprising because given by a young man whose mind and emotions appeared to be packed in ice. There was nothing to be gained by prolonging the interview. He stood up.

'I'm taking Becca and her mother to Italy in a few days' time.

My wife and I feel that a warmer climate and a change of scene will help restore her to full health . . . create a needed division between the recent past and the future. I shall come back as soon as they are settled, of course. It would give me both pleasure and some peace of mind if you found yourself able to come to Danesfield in the way you were used to do.'

Timothy stood too. Easily and evenly, he said, 'I do not go to Elswick as regularly as once I did, but if – when I do, I shall be happy to come to Danesfield.'

It had been a hopeless request. Nick had known it even while he spoke. If ever Timothy came, it would not be soon.

Relating what had passed at that meeting to Elise, Nick told her, 'He said nothing that allowed me to think that he felt more than friendship for Becca. Towards me, he behaved as graciously as a Spanish grandee and with as remote and unbending a pride. Since that damnable Sunday he seems to have aged twenty years. Not physically – in sophistication. At twenty-four years of age, he's formidable. And towards his father he is totally unforgiving. On that point he was unreachable, immovable, unnerving!' He stood in thought for a moment and then said, 'The two older sons may resemble Josh more closely in appearance, but in character it is Timothy who is nearest to what is essentially Josh. Easy-going, as both are, there is in them a dark intransigence which, though buried deep, when it surfaces, makes them reckless of all consequences. It was why when Andy was under threat from Captain Penn, the naval man, the only way to stop Josh putting his head in a hangman's noose was to put a bullet in him. Put Josh and Timothy in opposition and it is a case of God help them both! We haven't reached the end of it – and it is all through Becca!'

Josh! He appeared to them both as a looming problem but they found themselves unable to decide what was to be done.

As it happened, there was nothing they could do immediately. Josh had collected his crew and taken his newest lugger, *Joyous Lady*, to sea without making any attempt to contact either his friend or his youngest son.

CHAPTER FOUR

THE DAY AFTER the Mariotts left for Italy, Timothy received a letter from Rebecca. It was a short, formal note offering her apologies for any mischief done or vexation caused by her recent foolishness and thanking him for his generous help and support. Given the impossibility of her setting the facts down on paper, it made sense only to someone who knew to what she was referring. To Timothy, the voice of Nick Mariott sounded through every word.

He read it twice then fed it to the fire. For several minutes after he had watched it scorch and flare into extinction, he stood gazing down into the coals remembering his instinctive response to what he had recognized as Becca's dependence on his help. But would he have done it as unthinkingly as he had, he wondered, if he had known that the decision he made would divide him from his father and shut him off from so much of the life he had known? A satisfying life in which he had a foot in two worlds, the world of physical effort, of toil, adventure and warm family life on one side, and on the other, a wider world of ease and comfort, of knowledge, of literature and the arts, and of good conversation with familiar friends. Suddenly, his world had narrowed to the work he did in the small grey office at the Diment and Frewen premises and, a few hundred yards from them, time spent in these two unprepossessing rooms he occupied. He could expect occasional visits from his mother, he supposed, and more rarely, one or the other of his brothers. By comparison with what he had enjoyed, it was a lean and lonely prospect.

He knew himself to be self-sufficient to a large degree, but he would miss his brothers' rough and ready companionship and to some extent that of their wives and young families. Andy and Giles might tease and deride him for what they called his finicky manners and for his different way of speaking, but at the same time, he knew they held him in as warm affection as he did them: even Giles with his hasty and uncertain temper. They approved his readiness to help with the 'mucky' side of fishing when he could, and that they even boasted to others of the superior intelligence and learning of the young brother they pretended to despise. His home, with his mother at the heart of it, had been a warm and welcoming place ruled by the benign demi-god, his father. What he had lost could not be easily dismissed or forgotten. He could forgive Becca's lie told in dire need. It was not that which had severed him from the past. Unforgettably and unforgivably, it was his father's ready belief in it that had done that.

He remembered with fondness his first introduction to the 3-year-old Rebecca. . . . A small personality so dainty and pretty and female, so different from the pervading maleness of his own sisterless home, that he had immediately fallen slave to the miniature imperatrix. The years had brought the inevitable shifts in their relationship, elevating him to the role of elder brother with his own claims to command, but underneath there had remained an awareness of her female *otherness* and that her dependency conferred a responsibility on him: a responsibility that had never proved irksome.

Answering his own question, he knew that given the same choice with as much time as he needed to consider it, he would have responded as he had, and his certainty of that illuminated the reason. What had begun as a kind of boyish chivalry had, without his being aware, grown into a fully adult emotion of a different kind. The fact was that he loved and was in love with Rebecca Mariott and when marriage had been the answer to her extreme need, he had been able to discount the reason and find no sacrifice in offering that answer. It was now, when marriage was no longer a necessity to her, that it became a problem. Nick Mariott might accept Josh and his family on the level ground of equality in friendship, but when it came to the marriage of his daughter, without any compelling circumstance, he might not prove so liberally minded in the matter of who it was she married. As Timothy Ryland's wife, she would be stepping down from the position of a landed gentleman's daughter to the level of a man in trade and one who could offer her neither home, wealth or status. He, himself, wanted better for her.

What he felt for Rebecca Mariott, he decided, was something to be kept to himself.

The day after her return from the five weeks she had spent with her mother in Italy, Rebecca looked into her mirror and knew herself to be changed. Her face was thinner, perhaps even looked a little older. The open admiration shown her by Italian men and the generous, soundless handclap of the peasant women with their smiling, *Bella, bella!* had confirmed what her mirror told her. The knowledge that she was beautiful had given her more outward assurance than she once had. The journey, the splendours of the unknown country and the grandeur of its ruins had widened her horizons and she had been given time for the cruel edges of what had happened to her to be less constantly felt. What none of it had done was raise her self-respect.

This remained low. Despite all warnings, ignorance and foolishness had led to her falling easy victim to an unscrupulous man: ignorance and panic had then pushed her on to involve Timothy Ryland, drawing down on him, as she now knew, a good deal of unpleasantness from her father and his. Outrageously and without thought, she had relied on his supporting her claim that he was the father of her child but now, better informed, she could only wonder that he had done so, loyally and without hesitation. But in asking so much of him, had she had destroyed the friendship that meant so much to her? He had made no effort to write or to visit her since it had ceased to be necessary for her to marry, though her father, she knew, had done all that he could to put things right between them.

There was too, the puzzle of why, now the truth was known, he was still estranged from his family. Her mother told her it was a quarrel between Timothy and his father and it was not for her to pry into, but, from time to time, she wondered uneasily if she were not in some way to blame. Nannibet knew nothing about it, or Rebecca could have coaxed or prised the information out of her.

Even now she was not fully recovered from the shock of what had happened to her. Her nerves had been badly shaken, and for all her outward show, her inner confidence was undermined. With a deep sense of loss, she looked back to the safe and happy world of her childhood. The question of how she and Timothy were to meet also weighed on her mind. It could happen today . . . tomorrow . . . any time. She was sure the Ryland family were too closely bound in affection for them not resolve their differences before long. Then Timothy would resume his Sunday visits to his home – perhaps had already done so. Whatever happened, it was certain that if only by accident, she would meet him. The first occasion was bound to be difficult. In any family, the disgrace of a girl expecting a baby outside of marriage was something to be kept hidden from the rest of the world if at all possible, but she had made Timothy part of her shameful situation.

Society had an increasingly strict expectation of women's behaviour. It showed even in the clothes they wore; perhaps particularly in the clothes they wore. Looking at some of her mother's old gowns packed away in silver tissue, she could hardly believe they had been worn in public, so flimsy and lacking in material as they were – less even than would make a respectable shift today. And Elise had told her that when she was a girl daring young women had gone so far as to damp the skimpy muslins and silks of gowns and petticoats to make them cling to their figures all the more. There was a stricter morality abroad these days. If Timothy wanted nothing more to do with her, she should not be surprised. Yet, because they must meet some time, she tried to work through the muddle in her mind and decide how to conduct herself so that the occasion might pass with as little awkwardness as possible.

Before this good intention could progress further, it was all the greater shock to walk out of a shop in Chichester's South Street two days later and almost collide with Timothy who was returning to his office after calling on a client. Her nerves had not yet recovered their old resilience. Staring speechlessly at him, the blood rushed up to crimson her cheeks and then drained away to leave her pale and chill on the edge of fainting. Swaying, she stumbled, but before she could fall Timothy and Nannibet had sprung to her support. The Diment and Frewen's premises were only a short distance away and Timothy directed their footsteps to them. There was a small room on the ground floor furnished to impress the new or wealthier client with the firm's relaxed confidence in its reputation and achievements. Blessedly, it was unoccupied and Timothy was able to settle Rebecca in a comfortable chair and hurry off to find and bring her a glass of water.

A word with Mr Diment, the senior partner, brought that

impressive gentleman to pay his respects to the daughter of a valued client and when he was called away to attend another client, their small party was left in undisputed occupancy of the room for whatever time was needed.

As the weakness passed from her, Rebecca realized that the feared meeting had come about before she had prepared for it and she must carry it through as best she could. She took a quick look at Timothy through her lashes. He was looking grave and the formal clothes he was wearing made him look both older and more impressive. He was, she realized, no longer just the boy she had known from childhood, an extra and older brother to the two younger siblings presently away at school.

Screwing up her courage, she said to Nannibet, 'I need to speak privately to Mr Timothy, Nannibet, so will you leave us for a short while.'

Nannibet, weighing her incomplete knowledge of the involved story of the past few months against her duties as chaperon, decided it was a reasonable request and heaved to her feet.

'A little to your right, you will find a chair in a recess off the passage where you can be comfortable,' Timothy said, opening the door for her.

When he was seated opposite her again, Rebecca plunged nervously into speech. 'Timothy, I expect you received my letter, but I want to say how sorry I am properly. I did not realize what a dreadful thing I was doing when I said you were the – were the man. But with Mama away and Papa so angry— He said my disgrace would be public if I did not marry, that I would be ostracized and – and better off in a convent. I did not think beyond believing you would help me because you always had since I was little. And because we had been such good friends, I was foolish enough to think you wouldn't mind marrying me. Mama has helped me to understand better how very bad it was of me and how very disagreeable I made things for you. Can you forgive me?'

'It's all in the past now, Becca. I understood why you claimed I was the man involved. Don't think of it any more.'

Did he forgive her? He was sitting very upright, looking as though he wanted to be done with the subject; done with her apology and her thanks, too. The probability that she had lost not only his sympathy, but perhaps even his liking, brought tears into her eyes.

Breaking into nervous speech again, she said, 'I had been so looking forward to leaving school, putting my hair up, coming out, but – but everything turned horrid and now I feel so lost . . . so lonely.' She looked beseechingly at him, her lips trembling. 'Timothy, would you hold me the way you used to do when things went wrong? Just for a moment, to show you forgive me. It always comforted me . . . made me feel safe.'

'No, Becca, no!' He got hastily to his feet and walked as far away from her as the room allowed. 'That was when we were children, boy and girl, almost brother and sister. It's not like that any more. It would be' – he sought the right word and ended on a harsher note than he intended – 'unwise.'

'Oh.'

He sounded angry. She looked down at her hands lying clasped in her lap. 'I seem to go from bad to worse. Keep making silly mistakes . . . spoil everything. For you as well as me. Nannibet says you don't come to Elswick any more. Not even to visit your own home.'

'No,' he said shortly.

'Was that my doing, too?'

'No.' He lied without hesitation over that. 'I quarrelled with my father.'

'But quarrels end. People become friends again.'

'Not always.' He frowned. Shook his head. Said without meaning it, 'Perhaps I'll come to Danesfield one day.' He walked slowly back towards her. She looked so young, so vulnerable and so sweetly desirable that he knew he needed to bring their meeting to an end before he weakened and took her in his arms as she had asked, In a flat, purposeful voice he said, 'Now, how did you come into Chichester? By carriage?'

'Yes. It's at the livery stables in Mason Lane.'

'I'll send Nannibet in to you and find someone to go for the carriage. Excuse me.' He was out of the room before she could say more.

So brisk and determined an ending convinced her that he despised her. It was not surprising, she told herself She had used him . . . certainly that was how it must appear to him. But surely he understood? How could he turn away from her now when she needed him so much? Throughout her childhood, he had been her sure refuge when she was in trouble. To have his support withdrawn seemed to her like a betrayal.

She was still looking towards the doorway when Nannibet came through. Something in her expression made the woman say anxiously, 'What is it, my pet? What has happened?'

Rebecca seemed to withdraw her gaze from immense distance to refocus on the loving woman who had once been her nurse. 'Happened?' she repeated vaguely. Then with a dreary little smile, she said, 'Nothing, Nannibet, except that I think, slowly, little by little, I am beginning to grow up at last. And after all, Nanni, *I find I don't like it*!'

With Christmas only a few days away, Prue made another visit to her youngest son's office to point out to him that it was the season of goodwill and a good way to express it would be by spending all or part of the three-day holiday – it embraced the weekend – at home and making his peace with his father. She was unsuccessful. Timothy was unyielding in his refusal. Provoked, she demanded, 'What do you want from Josh before you'll come?'

'Nothing, Mama. That's what I seem unable to make you understand. I want *nothing* from him. As I have said before, for what he has given me in the past I am grateful. But he himself severed my past from my future . . . brought all that went to make up our former relationship to an end.'

'You surprise me, Timothy. You used not to be so hard.' She looked at him frowningly, said slowly, 'You're young. You've a lot of living to do. Time enough for you to make a mistake for which you'll be thankful to be shown some mercy . . . need forgiveness, perhaps.'

'If it happens – well, so be it! But if ever I have a son, I'll hope to think better of him – *know* him better – than my father knows me. If the man I am disappoints you too, Mother, I'm sorry. The pattern is set. I am that which I am. But' – he smiled darkly – 'what I am not, is the losel my father thinks me.'

Prue heard the tone with dismay. Pleaded, 'He knows he made a mistake where you are concerned, Son. It troubles him. But consider . . . are you without fault? Maybe you need to learn a little more of the value of humility.'

'The lesson in *humiliation* my father gave me recently should go some way towards it' His tone was barbed and bitter.

Defeated, Prue lapsed into silence, but then burst out again with, 'In the end, what will cutting yourself off from us all do for you? Will you be the better for that? Now? With Christmas almost upon us? What is it going to be like for you shut up in those two dismal rooms of yours by yourself?'

'I'll survive. Stop worrying yourself about me. I'm old enough to look after myself and you will hardly miss me in the crowd you will have around you with Andy and Giles, their wives and combined broods. Give them my good wishes. Don't work too hard. Let the younger women bear some of the burden.'

An invitation from Danesfield came so close on the heels of that abortive meeting as to make Timothy suspect collusion between the women of the two households. He declined it with careful courtesy. His sole share in Christmas cheer after that was to drink a glass of sherry with Mr Diment and Mr Frewen before the office was closed for the holiday . . . a holiday that seemed to him unnecessarily long before it ended.

CHAPTER FIVE

CONTRARY TO HIS own and Nick's expectations, Timothy went to Danesfield early in the New Year.

Nick was in the process of buying a house on his northern border that had recently been gutted by fire but to which was attached a useful acreage of land. Foolishly, the present owners had neglected to insure the property, could not afford to rebuild, and so were forced to move to an affordable house in Chichester. They needed a quick sale. Mr Diment was handling the transaction for Nick and completion was due in the second week of January when Mr Diment was to take the last papers to Danesfield to be signed and hand over the deeds. But Mr Diment had succumbed to a severe chill a few days before the appointment and Mr Frewen having important commitments of his own on that day, it was 'young Mr Ryland' who was called on to deputize for the senior partner.

Since the undertaking could not be avoided, Timothy set out for Elswick with resignation. The bleakness of the day did nothing to lift his mood. It was chilly and he rode at a fast clip along the bridleways and having handed his hired horse into the care of the groom who appeared, approached the house door with the memory of his last visit when Nick had poured out his angry contempt on him all too sharply alive in his mind. One could understand, excuse, forgive – forgetting was a different matter.

He hoped that this meeting would remain what it was intended to be, a matter of business and that personal relationships could be entirely disregarded. But the gods provide for their own amusement and, as he walked into the hall, Rebecca came into it from one of the nearby rooms. Both stood still, not speaking, uncertain how to take the moment past their very different recollections of the mood of their parting after their last meeting.

It was then that Timothy with some hastily formed idea of consolidating the distance he felt necessary to keep between them, said with small bow, 'Miss Mariott . . . good morning.'

Rebecca, wrestling with her own unhappy recollections of the disappointment and frustration of their last meeting, raised her head sharply. *Miss Mariott!* After all the years of being *Becca* to him. . . . Her grey gaze swept over him with glittering coldness and in an arctic tone, she responded, 'Mr Ryland. . . .' With the slightest of nods and an expressive swing of her skirts, she turned and walked out of sight through another door.

The bite of venom in her tone startled him, but conscious of the footman at his elbow waiting to conduct him to Nick, Timothy had no time to stop and think about it, the footman was opening the door into the library and of necessity, he walked through into the well-known room.

Nick had come half the length of it to greet his visitor and Timothy, answering the unspoken surprise on the other man's face, explained the reason for his presence in place of Mr Diment. That done, they settled to business at the handsome writing-table that through the years had served as Nick's desk. In less than half an hour the business had been completed and Nick was owner of twenty-two more acres and the shell of a once handsome house.

'You'll join us for lunch, of course?' Nick said then.

Hastily, Timothy declined. 'With Mr Diment away, we are hard pressed,' he excused himself. 'The season of goodwill being past, people are remembering their quarrels and discontents and turning to litigation, duelling now being a capital offence.'

'It was a barbaric resort in many cases, yet even now there are some willing to risk the penalties.'

'So I believe. But more and more care is needed to keep a meeting from being known about.' He grinned at Nick. 'It will die out completely before long, as every good lawyer must wish, litigation being good business even if it does mean our leisure is reduced.'

Nick accepted the excuse without attempting persuasion to set it aside. It would take time for anything like the old easiness between them to resurrect, he thought tolerantly. All one could do was have faith that it would. Through the years, the threads of his life and those of Josh and his sons, had twined and tangled. There had been checks and counterchecks, murder threatened and near murder done. But under all, against any and every probability, the bedrock of trust and interdependence on which the friendship was built remained unshaken. With the younger generation grown into adulthood, with their different natures, aims, passions and prejudices to complicate matters, Solomon himself might hesitate to attempt to resolve the problems that arose. And Josh was no help. Locked into an iron silence on the subject of Timothy and what had happened on a disastrous Sunday afternoon last September, he refused to discuss any detail of it. Prue had told Elise the ban held good in their own home: it was as though she and Josh had never had a third son, she said. Josh gave no recognition to Timothy's name, took no part in any conversation into which it was introduced. If any determined effort was made to break through the barrier, he simply left the room.

Josh might be refusing to acknowledge his youngest son's name, but by the end of May it Seemed that *Timothy Ryland* was on everyone's lips.

A case came before the courts in which law and justice stood all too plainly opposed. Through no fault of his own, James Jarrad stood to lose a great deal and all the sympathy that flowed his way could not alter the fact that, unfair as it was, the law was on the side of his opponent, Daniel Charlton. The best that Jarrad could hope for was that his solicitors might win for him the least injurious outcome from a poor choice and the firm of solicitors he had chosen for the task was that highly regarded local firm, Messrs Diment and Frewen. The two senior partners worked long and hard on reasons for mitigation, but were too experienced and too hard-headed not to accept that the case could not be won. The two gentlemen were not oblivious to the fact that however much sympathy a lost cause attracted, it did not pay to be seen as losers. Young Mr Ryland, so recently inducted into the firm, could be forgiven failure; could even attract a certain amount of sympathy on his own account as a young man making a valiant attempt at the impossible. With no thought of throwing him to the lions, his senior partners explained to him why they would be grateful if he would undertake to conduct the case.

Young Mr Ryland burned a great deal of midnight oil, read through the ancient print of old books on jurisprudence that appeared to hold anything, however remote, that might have a bearing on the case and fought his way through even more difficult cracklingly refractory parchment rolls of old briefs until his reddened eyes wept with self-pity.

In court, the prosecuting lawyers found themselves faced with fierce aggression where they had expected only barriers of defensive moves. The case was half over before they had regrouped. James Jarrad lost nothing that day. Materially, there was nothing he could gain. What he found himself with was a famous victory.

Timothy, as architect of that victory, found himself lifted out of obscurity overnight and all in a moment transformed into a man of promise, a young lawyer deserving respect and worth watching.

All he had to do, he told himself sardonically, was to prove he was capable of repeating his success. And even that began to appear a possibility as new clients presented themselves in gratifying numbers.

Neither Mr Diment nor Mr Frewen commented on the small use Mr Ryland had made of the facts, examples and precedences with which they had armed him but quietly went about making use of the enhanced reputation of the firm. The neat brass plate beside the entrance to the offices vanished for forty-eight hours and then reappeared amended to read, *Diment, Frewen and Ryland*. There were other changes: a small but handsome mahogany bookcase replaced the utilitarian bookshelves in the grey upstairs office and a cheerful red rug was laid before the visitor's chair in front of Mr Ryland's desk. Muted though the colour was, it introduced an almost frivolous note into the room's sobriety – or so Timothy was amused to think.

An unexpected outcome of the case was the opening up of his life outside the office. Seen as a rising star, he was invited to a number of social gatherings. Found to be an attractive, conversable and well-mannered young bachelor, hostesses were quick to recognize his value as a guest and before long he was in a position to pick and choose among his invitations.

It was September again when he met Rebecca at a ball given by one of the partnerships' wealthier clients. The house to which he had been bidden stood among trees in large grounds on the northern outskirts of Chichester where the land sloped gently upward at the beginning of its uneven climb to the Downs, He glimpsed her across the room early in the evening. She appeared to have come, not with her parents, but under the aegis of a pleasant-looking woman with a daughter of the same age: a school friend, he guessed. It was nearly an hour later before he found himself close to her.

He had just come in from taking a breath of fresh air on the terrace and she was not immediately aware of his presence. She was not alone. An escort of three young men vied for her attention and in the first moments he saw her as though through a stranger's eyes and not as a girl he had known from when she was a tot of three years.

The young woman he was looking at had come to full bloom and was dressed to complement it. Her full-skirted gown was white and frilled with delicate lace from hem almost to the waist. The lace was costly but wisely her jewellery was suited to her age, being no more than a modest pearl and peridot bracelet and a matching brooch centered in the swathed neckline of her gown from which her bare white shoulders rose in seductive perfection. Dressed by an expert, her glossy black hair formed a charming and highly fashionable arrangement around a small gilded wire ornament threaded with flowers.

Though they had not met, Timothy recognized the tall, fair-headed young man on her right hand as Lord Prescott's son and heir, Justin. Rebecca had entered her proper milieu, he thought with wry approval, determinedly ignoring the raking claws of jealousy. Deciding not to make an unwanted addition to Rebecca's court, Timothy turned away.

The movement caught her attention and she called to him, 'Mr Ryland, do not attempt to avoid us. Your fame has spread from Chichester even to the humble fishing villages. And as I and my friends are as fond of the company of the famous as anyone else, may I not for old acquaintance's sake, beg a moment or two of your time?'

Her assured tones suggested to him Rebecca had learned lessons in the months since he had last seen her. She spoke lightly, with the right, if misleading, hint of laughter in her voice, but clear to his ear was its knife-edged mockery. The last time she had spoken to him – at Danesfield, and just his name – there had been no subtlety in the way she had spoken: her tone had been as simple to understand as the rasp of a sword drawn purposefully from its scabbard. She had progressed beyond that, he judged – from sword to rapier. Now as then, he was the enemy. The glittering look that accompanied what she had just said, suggested to his mind that with an actual rapier in her hand, it would not be beyond her to smile as the steel slid into his living flesh.

She seemed almost to hate him and he still had not grasped how it had happened; how fifteen years of unfailing affection between them could be wiped away in a moment. That he had made a mistake when he had begun to address her as *Miss Mariott*, he realized, but surely that was not enough to destroy the bond between them? He recalled the way she had invited him to hold her when he had taken her to the Diment and Frewen offices. She had asked it with the same trust with which, as a child, she had always come to him for comfort when confronted by tragedy as when a kitten or a bird had died, or because of a heavy scold from her mama over some neglect or misdemeanour. From the earliest days he had spent at Danesfield, she had sensed his partisanship and relied on him to dispel her doubt that her tilting world would ever find its proper balance again.

But when – looking so young and so vulnerable – she had asked for comfort in the Chichester office he had been too newly awakened to the fact that his love for her was no longer that of a brother. When her lovely, tear-drowned grey eyes had looked at him and she had asked him to hold her as he had been used to do, he had known that if he had taken her into his arms then, he could not have put any reliance on himself to keep under control the boiling mix in him of love, pity and sheer murderous rage at what had been done to her.

It did not occur to him that the mischief between them was done then: that when he had set the length of the room between them, she had drawn from it a very different idea of why he done it than the true one. When, too, believing in the wisdom of putting their relationship on a more formal footing, he had addressed her as *Miss Mariott*, he could not know that it seemed only to confirm her belief that he had drawn back from her in disgust; that the use she had made of him in claiming him to be the father of her child, had destroyed his regard for her, cost her his respect. With a young and virtuous queen on the throne guided by an even more virtuous husband, the expectations of society leaned increasingly towards the absolute purity of its women, as became ever more plain to Becca. Because of what had happened to her she could no longer meet that standard of perfection. Unfair as it was, and rage against it as she did, she could not overcome the fact that in whatever circumstances a girl lost her virginity, society held her always to be at least partly to blame. That *Timothy* should subscribe to that view and apply it to her reduced her to a state of furious frustration. *He* – above all – should understand, should never, never, never think less of her!

Rebecca was introducing her escort now and Timothy forced himself to attend, but still the first two names escaped him entirely. Both young men congratulated him on his success in the Jarrad case without pretending to understand it. He did not expect it. The ramifications of the law were a mystery to most people, which was how, with a modicum of luck thrown in, lawyers grew rich. Rebecca introduced him to Justin Prescott last. With smiling intimacy, she said, 'I should have named Mr Ryland to you first, Mr Prescott, but you will care nothing for that, I know.'

Taking the hand held out to him, Timothy was aware that Prescott had used the intervening moments to make some sort of assessment of him.

'Ryland. . . .' Prescott said. 'I have it now. I could not for the moment place the name. You, like Portia, are the new Daniel come to judgement. "*O wise young judge, how I do honour thee*!'" His tone held only a hint of mockery but it was sufficient to allow Timothy to know Prescott was telling him he was not a man to be easily impressed.

' "*One swallow doth not a summer make*".' Secure in himself, Timothy quoted back, meeting Prescott's gaze with visible and amused indifference.

Prescott made a good recover. 'Yes. Sad, isn't it, to have to contemplate the need to prove oneself over and over again?' It was said with a smile that did not reach his eyes and Timothy knew that the difference between their prospects had been neatly drawn. Justin, as his father's heir, had no need to prove himself in any profession; his future was assured.

Rebecca's stony gaze caught his then, all their yesterdays seemingly forgotten, but Timothy was aware that she had recognized as clearly as Timothy himself what Prescott had been about. She had, he suspected, led the sacrificial lamb to the altar.

He looked at her with love and sadness and longed again to take her in his aims, not now for her comfort but his own. Longed to make wild, demanding love to her. . . . Instead, he conjured up an enigmatic smile, bowed and walked away.

With less sophistication than Timothy gave her credit for, Rebecca watched him go . . . hating him, hating Justin Prescott. But most of all hating herself.

CHAPTER SIX

A MONTH LATER Timothy was again at a ball. It was the grandest to which he had yet been invited and entering the handsome and brilliantly lit ballroom, he wondered how in the crowded room before him, he was to locate his host and hostess, the Earl and Countess of Ambershaw, both of whom were quite unknown to him. He was late, having been delayed by a fussy and over-anxious client, and the receiving line had been abandoned.

As he stood trying to decide in which direction to begin his search, a voice said in his ear, 'I knew it had to be you. I ran into Freddie Breasdale two days after my return from Germany and he told me about a young legal star that had risen in Chichester's heaven earlier this year. He was full of it because he was wondering if he could afford you to fight his looming battle over boundaries. I knew you lived somewhere near Chichester and I said it had to be you because you were bursting with brains and had studied law. And I was right!'

Timothy turned, recognized the pleasant, good-natured face of the young man who had spoken, bowed, and said formally, 'Lord Osmond.'

'God give me patience! Are you as stiff as ever? I swear you have more pride than Lucifer!' Osmond said, with a look of exasperation.

'*I!*' Timothy was astounded. 'What cause have I for a parade of pride?'

'Well, I don't know your circumstances, but the impression you give – have always given – is that nodcocks such as I am are far beneath your notice.'

Timothy laughed. 'You can only be speaking of our Oxford days and if I gave you that impression then, it was somewhat at a distance since you were a year ahead of me and reading Classics. Moreover, unless memory plays me false, I do not recall that they were handing out *firsts* to nodcocks when you took your finals.'

'My complaint is that having made your acquaintance, though I did what I could to show your company would be welcome, damn all response did I get. And unlike you, I was unable to distinguish myself by winning a string of prizes.'

Tmothy took the hand held out to him. 'You seemed always to have a great many people about you, but if, as it appears, I owe you an apology, I swear any offence I gave was unintentional, my lord.'

'And that's another thing – you can forget the title. I don't answer to it where I choose not. It is more than probable that you have forgotten my given name. My parents labelled me Peregrine, but my friends call me Perry. And there was no offence: only disappointment.'

'Thank you. My name you know and I have no rank to discard.' Timothy's crooked smile turned his lips, put a gleam in his eyes. 'All I can offer is that I come of a long line of seamen, none of whom has been hanged as yet for any smuggling activitivies in which they may have taken part.'

'Then we have more in common than I thought. Some day I will tell you how we came by our first honour. I promise you we were as fine a band of cut-throats as could be found.'

'A claim that, if honesty prevailed, could be made by half the nobility of the country.' Timothy swept a glance over the crowded room. 'What is concerning me at the moment is the lateness of my arrival and the difficulty of finding my unknown host and hostess. A garrulous client detained me and as I have not the least idea why I have been honoured with an invitation, or how the Earl and Countess of Ambershaw come to be aware of my existence, I have yet to make my bow to them.'

'You were invited because I asked them to invite you. They're my parents. How like you not to know! My barony's a courtesy title handed down to keep the eldest son happy. Or so it is supposed. Come with me and I'll—'

Breaking in on them, a voice said, 'I have just learned the name of your companion, Perry. I could hardly believe it! A friend of yours with brains! Introduce me at once, before he escapes you.'

Making room for the person who spoke, Perry said with a grin, 'This unmannerly hoyden I reluctantly bring to your notice, Timothy, is my sister, Lady Helena Osmond . . . Helena, Timothy Ryland.'

A pair of laughing hazel eyes met Timothy's. 'Mr Ryland, you have fallen not among thieves, but among philistines. I found my parents reeling from the shock of Perry having introduced a magus among us and had to come to view such a *lusus naturae* for myself.'

Timothy found himself facing a handsome young woman of 19 or 20, whose eyes fairly sparked with laughter as she held out her hand to him.Timothy took it and bowed over it. 'I fear you are bound to be disappointed. I benefit only by contrast with Perry.'

'What a damned unhandsome thing to say!' Perry protested. 'Only pistols at dawn will suffice to wipe out the insult. Er . . .' – he eyed Timothy with mock apprehension – 'or do your many skills include being a famous shot?'

'I do not care to boast, but—' Timothy returned grandly, never having handled a firearm in his life, but leaving the sentence unfinished to imply his expertise.

'Oh, Mr Ryland, I *do* like you. I thought you would be terribly stuffy. Don't give us up too soon, will you,' Helena implored him. 'We're all a little brighter than Perry.'

'He *is* stuffy. He has been calling me *Lord Osmond* and *my lord* in the most lowering way.'

'He is probably too polite to call you by the name that would more naturally leap to mind,' his sister threw at him before turning back to Timothy to say, 'Will you ask me to dance?'

'He hasn't met the parents yet. Better let him do the pretty first.'

'Oh, yes. But afterwards?'

'I shall be honoured—' Timothy began in answer and was immediately interrupted.

'*There*! If that don't prove he's stuffy! He could have been delighted . . . pleased . . . happy . . . but no, he's *honoured* to dance with a romp of a girl who happens, by my ill luck, to be my sister.'

'Ignore him,' Lady Helena advised Timothy. 'But bear with his presence until we have exhibited our prize to the parents. Then you and I may dance, if you will?'

One either side of him, with banter and laughter continuing, they guided him between and around guests, until they came to a halt before an older man and woman standing talking to a very elderly woman seated in a thronelike chair. There was enough likeness between Perry and the man for Timothy to guess they had reached the Earl and Countess of Ambershaw. Introductions informed him that the very elderly woman was the Dowager Countess.

They stood chatting for several minutes, but then as others came to join the group, Timothy and the two junior Osmonds took their leave. As they turned away, the Dowager asked in the overloud tones of the deaf, '*Who* did you say that handsome young fellah is?'

'Timothy Ryland,' the earl told her. 'The young lawyer everyone's talking about.'

'Ryland . . . Ryland. . . . Don't know any. Newcomers, maybe. . . . What's certain is, that one's far too handsome for his own good. And what's more than certain is, he's far too handsome for any *gel's* good. You'd better keep a watchful eye on that flighty daughter of yours, Gerard.'

The younger people were still within earshot, but pulling Timothy towards the dance floor and giving him no time for embarrassment, Lady Helena said with a laugh, 'Come on, my handsome young fellah, you are contracted to dance with Gerard's flighty daughter so let us join the merry throng.'

It was noon three days later when Timothy took a short cut through a passage linking Chichester's East Street with the road he wanted. Crossing its packed-earth surface to the far side, he became aware of a man watching him from the doorway of the corn-chandler's store. A moment later, he realized the man was Josh. It was almost a year since he had seen his father and stepping on to the narrow, cobbled pavement, he was looking directly at him. Turning in the direction he wanted, he touched the brim of his hat, said, 'Sir,' and with no flicker of change in his stony expression, walked on. It was a brutally minimal acknowledgement of an unwanted connection, and what courtesy there was in it had the bite of a keen-edged blade slipped between the ribs.

For a moment Josh stared after him, then he turned and went deeper into the dim, dusty interior of the store.

October came in on a blast of cold air that was an all too sharp reminder that winter was not far off. Late in the month, with the harvest safely in and Josh returned from a successful fishing trip two days before, he sat with Nick Mariott by the fire in the bookroom at Danesfield with tankards of Danesfield's best home-brewed at their elbows, indulging in a morning idleness unusual to both. This kind of occasional, informal and *tête-à-tête* hospitality was the only kind Josh ever accepted from Nick.

Stretching his legs towards the blazing coals, Nick said meditatively, with no deliberate intention, 'I see Timothy again distinguished himself in court last Thursday by winning record compensation for the Remmingtons.'

Josh grunted unintelligibly, sharpening Nick's attention. He looked at his friend's closed expression and said, 'Josh, you cannot go on pretending that Timothy has dropped out of existence. The break between you has been going on too long. It is wrong and I cannot stand by and let the matter rest without doing something towards putting things right. How can I allow you to lose your youngest son through me or mine? What happened between you and Timothy was because of the false claim Rebecca made. Morally and under the law, I am responsible for what my under-age daughter does and says. If there is something I can do to put things right, I can only beg you to *tell* me.'

Josh's expression remained unchanged, his still brilliantly blue eyes hooded. He said, 'There's nothing you can do, Nick. You can take the blame for Becca if you must, but you can't take the blame for what *I* did. And what is worse, for what I did *not* do. *That's* what chafes Timothy most. But the past is out of reach; it can't be undone or redone. Let it go.'

'I cannot. It troubles my conscience. Timothy is a reasonable and mature young man. . . . Surely if I—'

'I'll tell you this and it's the last I'll say on the subject,' Josh cut in impatiently. 'Something more than a week ago he passed within two feet of me. . . .' He told Nick what had happened in Chichester and before the other man could comment said, 'What do I do now? Apologize? *How*, if he won't listen? And he won't! In his shoes, nor would I! I used the unfair advantage of my greater strength to make him choose between standing to take a thrashing or being tied and forced to take it. He knew he was boxed in and I watched him decide. He laid no claim to innocence at that point. And that could only be because he decided I was in no mood to listen. He was probably right. Giving me no answer, he simply took off his coat and shirt and strolled to stand where I told him. There, he stood and stared at me for a moment, then humped his shoulders, curled his lip and invited me to do what he could not prevent me doing. The manner in which he did it, more or less encouraged me to do my worst. I obliged him by doing just that – more or less!' He kept a moment's black silence, remembering, shook his head and continued, 'Nick, never before had I flogged man or beast Why did I have to wait until my youngest son reached manhood to start? And not a sound did I wring out of him except for one cry at the beginning when I laid the lash across his back before he was expecting it. Unfairly, as I knew, quietening my conscience with the belief that he had earned it. So he had. He had offended my pride . . . though a more honest name for it might be vanity. None of the three boys had ever looked at me as he did at that time. It was more than I could tolerate and I'll admit to you what I have barely admitted to myself, that part of the punishment I gave him that day was for that.'

He lapsed into silence again and into even blacker contemplation of what had reft his youngest son from him before adding, 'I believe he'd have let me flog him unconscious rather than utter another sound after that beginning. And then to find he had nothing to do with Becca's plight—!' He looked across at Nick. 'I'm not proud of myself, but I tell you, Nick, the boy did his share towards putting my feet on the wrong path!'

'He's not a boy, Josh: he's a man and a clever one.'

'He has made sure I know it! But bad as it was, it wasn't the thrashing that choked him, it was my failure to ask him if what Becca said was true. As sure as fate, if I *had* asked, at that time, for Becca's sake, he would have lied and said *yes*. But I would have *asked*. That was where I lost him. As assuredly as if he had died.'

'But I failed him on the same point'

'You're Rebecca's father. He thought it natural that you accepted her word; as why shouldn't you? He expected at least a *doubt* of his guilt from me and he didn't get it. So I say again, Nick – let be! It's too late.'

With summer at an end, the pleasures of autumn came in pell-mell before winter could lay its forbidding hand on easy travel. For the men there was shooting and hunting: the ladies had their evening parties, balls and visits to the theatre to crowd in before the weather made even short journeys hazardous.

In the villages, groups of friends and neighbours shared carriages to go to both private balls and those at the Assembly Rooms in Chichester and elsewhere. If Elise and Nick needed any proof of their daughter's popularity, they were given it in abundance. Foremost among her beaux was Justin Prescott. Nick, watching his lovely daughter's careless acceptance of the young man's attentions, wondered if she realized that Prescott's manner towards her was becoming increasingly proprietorial. He was not surprised, when a week or two before Christmas, Prescott sought a meeting with him and asked for permission to address himself to Rebecca with a view to marriage.

There was no reason Nick could think of to withhold it. The young man was heir to a long-established barony, the family was well-to-do and stable, and he knew nothing that detracted in the least from Prescott's character. How well Rebecca liked him, he did not know. He neither particularly liked nor disliked the young man himself and so granted his request, warning him only, 'You have my permission to speak to Rebecca when you feel the time is right, but please understand that the decision to accept or decline your offer rests with her. I foresee no happiness in matches that are made under parental constraint.'

Prescott had little expectation of failing of his object, which made his rejection more of a shock than it otherwise would have been. Adding to his shock was Rebecca's obvious surprise, as though it had not occurred to her that his attendance on her through the past weeks could lead to this end. Conscious of his own worth, Prescott considered the indignation he felt justified.

CHAPTER SEVEN

TIMOTHY DID NOT expect the Osmonds' interest to last beyond the evening of the Ambershaw ball. Their way of life would be too different from his and even accidental meetings were improbable. He wrote his bread-and-butter letter to his hostess and considered that the end of the matter, just something to be stored among his more pleasant and amusing memories.

He was wrong in his estimation of the Osmonds' interest however. Before many days had passed, with tact and grace, Perry Osmond had suggested a meeting between them at an hour that recognized the claims of business on Timothy's time without appearing to notice them. Other such meetings followed. They shared a certain irreverence of outlook which both, for their different reasons, were compelled to keep generally under restraint. The freedom to exchange the occasionally ribald point of view without being misunderstood or having to explain allusions was a relief to two lively minds. Now and then, their meetings were made into a threesome by the addition of Lady Helena who showed herself to be as relaxed and pleasant in everyday life as she had been at the ball.

On a Saturday early in December, with her usual charm of manner, the Countess of Ambershaw, well wrapped in furs, performed the opening ceremony at a charity market held in

East Street in aid of two local orphanages and several other charities. All goods offered for sale had been donated and the event was well attended by the many who came in the hope of finding bargains. Neither of the Countess's children felt obliged to attend the opening, but they arrived a little before four o'clock, soon after the naphtha flares had been lit.

Four o'clock was the official hour at which, on this day of the week, the offices of Messrs Dimont, Frewen and Ryland closed for the weekend, but that time was frequently ignored if pressure of business required it. On this particular Saturday, Perry, making shameless use of his rank, sent in his card and let it be known Mr Ryland's attention to a matter of business was urgently required. Consequently, Timothy found himself leaving the premises at no more than a few minutes past the hour in the company of Perry Osmond and his sister.

The two Osmonds had walked through the charity market – to which they were all now headed back – on their way to Timothy's office. Perry had little to say about the goods on offer beyond supposing that they would have to buy *something* to contribute to its success. Given the cue by his sister, he had rather more to say about a girl he had seen.

'The most glorious creature you ever saw, Timothy. Here with her maid, or some such I should think.'

'And who is this nonpareil?'

'That is what I do not know and probably never shall. I expect they've gone by now.' He sighed. 'That Byron thing just about sums her up.'

'*Which* Byron thing?'

'Oh, the one that says something about her walking in beauty like the night of . . . um . . . starry skies and . . . er . . . clouds and things.'

' "*She walks in beauty like the night of cloudless climes and starry skies; And all that's best of dark and bright meet in her aspect and her eyes*",' Timothy supplied, though he suspected Perry knew the poem as well as he did.

'That's it! But can you give her a name?'

Timothy laughed. 'From that? I might supply three or four and still not give you the one you want.'

'He saw her only for a moment or two . . . just long enough to earn a well-deserved glare from the dragoness guarding her,' Lady Helena scoffed. 'In a good light he'd probably discover she has freckles and a cast in one eye. She was wearing one of the new Hungarian cloaks, too, which hide a multitude of figure faults. I'll allow it appeared to be lined with chinchilla so she may be well-endowed with worldly goods . . . though even that could be a take-in and the fur no more than rabbit or cat.'

'The sooner the parents ship you off to London to acquire a little town polish, my girl, the better I shall like it,' her brother told her blightingly.

Helena laughed but allowed the subject to drop.

Dutifully, they bought a number of small items not too cumbersome to carry and began making their way through the crowd towards South Street where Perry's tilbury waited for them in charge of his groom. Timothy stopped at a bookstall he had not yet visited and the other two moved to the next stall selling bric-à-brac. Having bought a nicely bound edition of Virgil's *Eclogues* that had caught his eye, Timothy turned from the stall to find himself face to face with Rebecca and close behind her, hovering like a plump guardian angel, Nannibet laden with packages.

Taken by surprise, Timothy said on a note of pleasure, 'Becca—' and then hurriedly, more formally, with a slight bow, 'Miss Mariott. . . .' while bestowing a smile and a nod on Nannibet. It was months since their last meeting and he tried to recollect the details of it while his eyes drank in Becca's loved and lovely features. It had been late last year, he recalled, at a ball given by a client. It had not been a happy meeting. Yet here, in the first moment of recognition, he could have sworn she had been pleased to see him. It must have been wishful thinking because already her brows were drawing together, her eyes were gathering storm light and gazing at him with cold disdain.

Before he could decide what his next step was to be, there was an urgent tug on the back of his coat and Perry's voice said, 'Will you not present me to your friend. . . ?'

It was then he realized that the cloak Becca wore fitted the description Lady Helena had given of the one worn by the dark beauty who had inspired Perry to wax lyrical. Stifling an upsurge of reluctance, Timothy said, 'Miss Mariott, may I present Lord Osmond . . . Perry, Miss Mariott.' And then, as Helena joined them, extended the introduction to include her.

Becca flashed him a half-startled glance before acknowledging the introductions. However maladroit her relations with him might be, her company mannners were easy and graceful and within a few minutes they were strolling together among the last of the stalls and had reached agreement that they had seen as much as they wished of the charity market and began to move towards the Mariott carriage waiting in South Street. There, Timothy stood back to allow Perry the privilege of handing Rebecca into the vehicle with careful gallantry, a courtesy he accorded Nannibet with equal grace. Their goodbyes said, the remaining three walked on to where the Osmonds' chaise waited further along the same street, Timothy answering a spate of questions from Perry regarding Miss Mariott. From these Perry learned that Timothy knew her because she was a neighbour, had known her almost since her cradle days, his carefully maintained tone of cheerful unconcern conveying, as he intended, that she held no special interest for him.

'Don't you think her the most beautiful girl you have ever seen?' Perry asked eventually, as though unable to believe that any man could escape thinking so.

'Well, I know that for some time she has been considered

exceptionally handsome,' Timothy conceded with slow deliberation, as though he had never given the point any particular consideration, 'but you must remember I knew her in her gap-toothed childhood and as a skinny schoolgirl. Those things leave their impression, too. I supppose she is as pretty as any girl I can at present bring to mind.'

'Pretty!' Perry snorted indignantly. 'You have neither eyes to see with, nor soul to appreciate beauty when it stands before you!'

They arrived at the Osmonds' chaise just then and Timothy found himself unexpectedly glad to part with them and was firm in declining all invitations to accompany them to Ambershaws.

He walked the short distance to his rooms in gloomy thoughtfulness, dwelling on the difference between what he and Perry could offer Becca if the attraction she had awoken in him lasted. If it came to marriage, he could offer her the prospect of high rank, membership of an ancient family and greater wealth even than she presently enjoyed. In time, she would be promoted to being mistress of more than one handsome property and be blessed with a husband as good-natured as he was personable. In contrast, all he, Timothy, could put forward was the occupancy of two rather dreary rented rooms and perhaps eventually a very ordinarily comfortable income. . . .

Shortly after six on a cold, sleety evening, with another Christmas seemingly having crept up on him, Timothy returned to his rooms at the end of a busy day, looking forward to building up his sitting-room fire to a comforting warmth and sitting before it with a glass of brandy and hot water to enjoy the luxury of doing nothing except make up his mind at which of the nearby hostelries he would dine. His landlord, meeting him in the narrow passage that led from the door of the house, put this programme in suspension.

'Visitor waiting for you upstairs. Claimed he was your

brother so I let him in.' The old man shuffled uneasily, uncertain he had done right, but unwilling to explain that the visitor's size and the firmness of his intention to enter the house had made opposition to that intention appear unwise.

'Tall and tow-headed?' Timothy asked.

' 'Sright,' the old man nodded.

'My brother,' Timothy said.

He went upstairs eagerly, two at a time. Either brother meant news from home, the link every exile craved.

The lamp had been lit and the fire built up making his living-room bright and as welcoming as its grey drabness allowed. It was Andy, his elder brother, ten years his senior, who lifted his large figure from the chair in which he had been sitting and turned to look at him. For several moments they stood assessing the changes that had come to them in the months since they had last seen one another. Andy's unsmiling gaze held Timothy in the doorway, his own smile fading. The blue gaze, so similar to Josh's, washed down over the dark frock-coat and grey watered-silk waistcoat his younger brother was wearing, before rising again to meet the green of his gaze.

'Well, Tim,' he said at last, 'a man of affairs and quite the gentleman these days, aren't you? I shall find myself having to call you Mr Ryland before long.'

Timothy's dark brows drew together. Smothering his disappointment, he stepped into the room and closed the door behind him. 'Are you here to quarrel with me, Andy?' he asked quietly.

'Not to begin with. Though it will surprise me none if it ends that way.' Truculence edged Andy's tone.

'Very well. Make your point.'

'It's simple enough . . . are you coming home at all this Christmas?'

'*Your* home, Andy?'

'You know what I mean – the old folk.'

'My father's house then. . . . No. I shall not be going there.'

Andy made a sound of exasperation. 'What the hell happened between you and the old man? Why is it such a black secret? Pa won't tell me, yet Ma knows. But she won't tell me either. I've half a mind to beat it out of *you*, except that Ma would probably light into me with a skillet if I spoiled your pretty face.'

'And you would be none the wiser for having done it.'

Andy's clenched hands and smouldering look showed how strongly tempted he was to put that issue to the test. He said, 'You might be wrong about that if I really set about you. Though I'll grant you were always a mule-headed brat, too stupid to know when to give in, more ready to get yourself knocked senseless than yield to reason!' He gave the nearby table an exasperated thump. 'It's Ma being unhappy because her youngest nestling don't visit that brings me here. Knowing how resty it makes Pa when Ma's upset, it's a world's wonder he hasn't hauled you home to her by the scruff of your neck before this.'

Puzzled and scowling, he stared at his younger brother. 'That he hasn't, doesn't make sense. It isn't like him. Maybe he's getting old, hard though that is to believe. But he *is* past sixty and since things are as they are, I'm here to tell you it's past time you apologized for whatever you said or did that put Pa out. Even if he barred you from home then, he can't have meant it to last forever and he'll let you back aboard if only for Ma's sake. If it's so bad you have to crawl, and it's sticking in your craw, well, you should have thought of that before you made him show his teeth.'

Timothy's green eyes, intent and brilliant, narrowed on him. 'Fine advice, big brother, if it fitted!' he said derisively. 'What if the boot's on the other foot? Do you think Father will crawl to me? Particularly knowing – as I assure you he does – that he'll win no pardon from me, even for my mother's sake. Mother may fret, but she understands.'

Andy stared at him. 'Are you saying it was that way round?' He shook his head. 'No. I don't believe it! Short of gelding you, what could Pa ever do to you to give you the right to come the high admiral over him?'

Timothy stiffened. Thin-lipped and cold-eyed, he left the question unanswered.

Andy's scowl deepened. 'Grown too big for your boots . . . that's more the size of it! Maybe you *need* a hiding and I should forget the nonsense about it being no fair match. It could make for more comfort in the family and even do you some good.'

'Decide as you please. The end will be what it's always been.'

'It's all that holds me back, damn you! Why cannot you give me a hint of what the trouble is between you and the old man? I'm not likely to pass it to the town crier and I could maybe help.'

'No. It's between my father and myself. Since nothing will – nothing *can* – change it, you'll do better to leave it alone, Andy.' The words fell flat but positive between them.

'Ma won't let it rest.'

'Mother's done all that's in her power. The breach is between my father and myself and is unlikely to be bridged.'

'You've let Ma plead without heeding her?' Andy glared, his anger visibly climbing the scale. 'Ma, Pa – their best is what they've always done: for you, for me, for Giles. If that don't count with you, then go to hell, I've done with you! I'll go while I'm still able to keep my hands off you. You won't see me here again and you'll find no welcome in my house. You're no brother of mine!'

Pushing past Timothy on his way to the door, he opened it, paused, and threw back over his shoulder. 'You might get a visit from Giles. Remember he burns a shorter fuse than I do. He might forget you're the runt of the family and have to be treated with special care. If he does, he'll get no blame from me!' He jerked the door closed behind him, there was a brief thump of boots on the stairs followed by the slam of the house door.

The tinny little clock on the mantel seemed to tick louder after that, as though trying to fill the heavy silence. It was only when, with a gasp and a whirr, it struck seven high, thin notes that Timothy stirred. Crossing to a cupboard, he took from it a glass and a decanter and poured out a stiff measure of the golden liquid. Half-raising the glass towards the door, wryly bitter, he said, 'A happy Christmas to you, big brother!' and tossed the liquor down.

CHAPTER EIGHT

CHRISTMAS PASSED AS bleak and unfestive as had been the last one as far as Timothy was concerned. He excused himself from accepting an invitation from Perry to join a house party at Ambershaws, unwilling to chance inflicting the least hurt on his mother if, hearing of it, she thought he preferred that invitation to hers. The best that could be said of the four long empty days was that they brought him no visit from Giles.

The short, dark days of the New Year were bedevilled by squalls as erratic in their suddenness as the outbreaks of unrest throughout the world. Ireland was once again in a state of disquiet and trouble threatened among the Sikhs in the Punjab; in France, discontent with Louis Phillipe was growing and revolution seemed to be impending in half the capitals of Europe. It looked as though the year ahead was to be an uneasy one.

In the the first week in February, Timothy was again summoned to Elswick. Not this time, however, to Danesfield.

Two years previously Elswick had lost the benign magistrate who had served it for so long when Sir Roland Anstey had died of a heart attack. Lady Anstey, genuinely heartbroken, had sold the manor house eighteen months later and gone to live with an unmarried cousin in Dorset. The manor was now owned and occupied by a wealthy family named Lasseter who, with a son of seventeen and twin girls aged twelve, pleased the neighbourhood by adopting as though inherited, the Anstey tradition of chief party and ball-givers to the locality. If these occasions had not yet arisen quite so frequently as they had in the Ansteys' day, some compensation was to be found in the sheer lavishness of the arrangements when they did.

Rupert Lasseter, head of the family and new to the neighbourhood, found himself in need of a local man of business, heard the name of Timothy Ryland mentioned several times as the up-and-coming man and made a point of meeting him Surprised by his youth, he hesitated: his affairs were complex and required skilful handling. The speed and ease with which Timothy grasped the information he was given together with what was expected or hoped for in return for outlay, decided Lasseter to give the young man a trial. He placed no more than a portion of his business concerns in Timothy's hands to begin with, but that portion was not unimportant and he waited through the following months ready to step in and take over at the least sign of incompetence. He was more than satisfied when he found there was none.

With Timothy having little leisure, Perry found his own way of extending his acquaintance with Rebecca Mariott. Working his way through the friend of a friend of a friend, he found out which were the families who had some acquaintance with the Mariotts and put himself in the way of being invited to such parties and entertainments that held out a reasonable hope of his meeting Miss Mariott there. When this occurred, he made ruthless use of his sister in promoting friendship between the three of them. And having made the acquaintance of the young lady's parents, did all in his power to improve upon it.

It was Timothy's misfortune that Perry elected him confidant-in-chief and he was forced to listen to many a panegyric on Becca's perfections. His attempts to head Perry off received little attention, Perry placing comfortable reliance on his memory of the lack of interest Timothy had displayed in Miss Mariott after introducing them.

Timothy did not find it easy to stand aside while another man wooed the girl he loved. For the first time in his life he experienced feelings of envy and jealousy of which he was ashamed. He told himself that Becca deserved the good fortune of making an exceptional match after the ill luck that had attended her entry into adult society. Certainly the marriage of Miss Mariott to the future Earl of Ambershaw – if that was what it came to – would be looked on by the world as a brilliant match for a country gentleman's daughter. With a clear field and Perry at his charming best, Timothy could not see how it could fail to happen unless the earl, his father, chose to step in and put an end to his son's association with a young woman who, though a gentleman's daughter, was not of their own order.

For her own reasons, Lady Helena aided and abetted her brother's pursuit of his dark-haired beauty and mid-summer Sundays quite frequently found them engaged with Timothy in some amusement as a foursome.

Timothy's easy relationship with the Osmond brother and sister had again brought to Rebecca's attention that her view of him must be enlarged to take in that he was visibly rising in the world. She thought it perverse that it did not act to draw them closer, but seemed to push them further apart, with Timothy resigning her to Perry Osmond without any sign of regret. Her resentment was deepened by the speed with which easy friendliness grew between him and Lady Helena and her suspicion that that young lady's interest in him needed only encouragement to move beyond friendship.

Among the present Earl's interests was breeding a particular line of hunters. They began life at Ambershaws, were broken and schooled there before being moved to other of his estates until they were ready to be sold.. On a damp and windy Sunday in mid-April, the younger Osmonds were with

Timothy and Becca in the wet-weather schooling barn, amusing themselves with a not very earnest archery contest. Timothy and Helena were standing side by side, leaning on the rail that separated them from the central tan on which the targets had been set up, watching Perry correct Rebecca's aim and stance. Becca loosed an arrow which hit the canvas but without entering any of the roundels of the target. Patiently, Perry demonstrated her errors and Becca's next arrow did very much better.

With a laugh and a shake of his head, Timothy said, 'I cannot think why any of us enter into contest with Perry when marksmanship is involved. His eye and aim have an accuracy hard to match.'

'Yes,' Helena agreed lightly. 'As it is with arrows, so it is with guns: what he aims at, he hits. I almost feel sorry for the game, they stand so little chance.' She was silent for a moment or two and then, abruptly sober, said, 'Already, he's more than halfway serious about Rebecca, you know.'

'Yes. So I think,' Timothy agreed, his voice carefully expressionless.

Helena moved restlessly. 'I have not seen him in such purposeful pursuit of a girl before. It troubles me because, for all his fooling, Perry's feelings run deep and I do not think Miss Mariott feels for him as he feels for her. Or is even aware of having awakened such feelings in him. I hope she will not hurt him.'

'Rebecca would never do so intentionally.'

'No. But between men and women it can happen without intention.'

'It's a risk we all take.'

Helena sighed. 'You are right, of course, but I wish Perry were less vulnerable. As I said, he feels deeply and though rarely angry, when he is, his anger is black, cold, deadly – and lasting. I have sometimes thought that at such times he could be dangerous.'

'You do not surprise me . . . "*Beware the fury of a patient man*". . . .'

'Yes. That is precisely what I mean.' She gave him a long considering look. 'What is more, I suspect you have a similar disposition. And now I am going to risk asking a question I have no right to ask. I shall not take offence if you refuse to answer. You have every right to do so.' She drew breath. 'Miss Mariott – sometimes you look at her in a way that makes me wonder if Perry is right in thinking you have no more than friendly feelings for her.'

'If that is a question then I have no difficulty in admitting I feel more for her than mere everyday friendship,' Timothy said. He spoke lightly, intending to mislead. 'I have known her since she was three years old . . . spent many of my school holidays in her home when my family were living in France . . . watched her grow up. She is almost but not quite a sister.'

She gave him a sharp look and a wry smile. 'I am answered and not answered,' she said.

'Don't make too much of it. At present, if my feelings for a woman led me to thoughts of marriage, it would be beyond me to make any sort of an offer that could interest her, or which any parent or guardian would think worth two minutes' consideration. I am a man who works for his living and who has everything to do. It will be ten years at least before I can think of marriage.'

'A rich wife would answer your problem.'

'She would need to want very little in return to accept a man without standing or connections, the son of a seaman. Also one just starting out on his career, having no house, just two rather dreary rented rooms. I do not fancy having to put my chances to the test with any sensible woman.'

'Women in love are rarely sensible. You might be lucky.'

He was saved from responding to that by the other two calling to them that it was their turn to address the bull's-eye.

Rebecca Mariott's rejection of Julian Prescott's proposal had continued to ruffle that gentleman's feelings. To have a truly beautiful wife whom other men would covet contributed to Prescott's picture of himself and his standing among men. At the Mayday Ball held at the Assembly Rooms in Chichester which they separately attended – Rebecca under her mother's chaperonage – Rebecca's obvious popularity reactivated Prescott's interest. Having secured a waltz with her, he exerted as much charm as he was capable of and afterwards carefully steered her into one of the small private rooms beyond the ballroom. There, drawing her to a halt, he said softly, 'Rebecca . . . Miss Mariott . . . I have not . . . *cannot* give up hope. So I am asking you again if there is a chance that your feelings may have changed – warmed – towards me since last I spoke to you of marriage? *My* feelings run too deep for me to give up hope easily. I would do all in my power to make you happy if you would only consent to marry me.'

Rebecca had thought the idea of marriage between them had been safely left behind. Far from flattering her, she was embarrassed by his persistence and because of it there was a hint of impatience in her tone when she said, 'I had hoped the subject of marriage between us was closed, Mr Prescott. Your friendship I value, but my feelings for you do not go beyond friendship. Please accept what I say and save us both further embarrassment.'

He could not immediately believe that she was refusing him a second time. He was offering her an assured position, an old family name and title, backed by profitable estates and wealth equal to, if not surpassing, that of her own family. He was not practised in restraint and following a long moment of silence, his hands gripped her shoulders and he was shaking her so violently that the pins flew from her coiled hair so that it fell like glossy black silk over her face and neck.

'You led me on. Gave me every encouragement. You're a cheat and a flirt. No better than a common harlot. . . .' Words poured from him, his injured pride driving him beyond reason so that the tirade went on and on.

Rebecca, dizzy from the shaking, was helpless in his hands and when it suddenly ended and he strode from the room, she sank to the floor as though boneless.

Traumatic as her experience had been with Edward Jordan and what followed from that, no one had ever before laid hands on her in such way or used such language towards her and she was too shocked to hold back her tears.

Elise Mariott, unable to see her daughter in the ballroom, was relieved to see Timothy and enlisted his help in finding her. Walking along the passage from which some of the lesser rooms led off he glanced through an open doorway and was at once halted. In a moment he was kneeling beside the figure huddled on the floor racked with shuddering sobs.

'Becca!' The depth of her distress put everything else out of his mind. Almost afraid to touch her, he stroked her tangled hair, said tenderly, 'Becca, my dearest girl, it's Timothy. What has happened?'

Too choked by tears to speak, she could only shake her head.

'Come. Stand up.' He stood himself and pulled her up with him. 'Tell me what has happened and why your hair is flying all about you like this.'

Instinctively, she responded to the lure of the old source of comfort and turning into his aims, hid her face against his shoulder. As unthinkingly, his arms closed round her in the way they always had when she was in trouble. She pressed closely into her longed-for refuge and haltingly, told him of having declined Prescott's offer of marriage nearly two months ago and of the grudge he must have held and allowed to break out this evening following a second refusal.

'He shook me until my hair fell down and he said such things. . . . Oh, Timothy, I did not lead him on! I had no idea he was thinking of marrying me until he first proposed to me.' She burrowed her head into his shoulder and clutched at his lapels. 'Nothing has gone right since I left school. Everything is so different from what I thought it would be. I don't understand! Even you—'

'The adult world can be a rough place, Becca. The rules are more complex. Even I cannot behave towards you as I did when I spent my school holidays at Danesfield.' It occurred to him that it was just what he was doing and he eased her gently away from him, conscious that the door of the room remained wide open and anyone passing might look in on them and make what they chose of what they saw.

'Oh, don't push me away!' She tried to cling to her position, but Timothy was firm.

'It is one of the first rules, Becca. Unmarried and unrelated men and women, do not hold each other as we have been doing unless—' Hastily he abandoned the end of the sentence . . . *unless they are engaged to be married.*

Hurt and disappointed, she said, 'I suppose I am embarrassing you?'

'Well, yes. You are.' *In several ways, one of which is unlikely to occur to you*, he thought wryly.

'I see.' The hurt deepened, woke a spark of angry pride. Her head lifted. 'I'm sorry.' With an effort, she stood back from him. Casting a wandering glance round the room, as though repeating a lesson she said, 'I must look for my pins and tidy myself. There is a mirror over the fireplace and I have a comb.' Her gaze came back to him. With further effort, half angrily, she said, 'What a nuisance I am to you. But I am all right now. Perhaps you would shut the door as you go out.'

'Good girl,' he said, encouragingly. 'You'll manage. Don't take any notice of anything Prescott said. He's just a poor loser. I'll wait for you outside. Your mother asked me to take you to her.' He took one of her hands in his and raised it briefly to his lips. The next moment he was gone, closing the door after him as she had asked.

Rebecca stood unmoving for several long moments. Why could she not learn? The past was past and she only embarrassed Timothy by wanting to return to it. He was trying to end their old relationship gently amd kindly and must find her unwillingness very tiresome. She had learned that what had happened to her at her come-out party was enough to give any man a disgust of her. She knew now, that unfair as it was, a girl who lost her virginity even by rape, was held to be in some way at fault Beyond that, it would be no wonder if the lie she had told naming him as the man responsible had made him hate her. Perhaps he did. . . . Yet he had made neither denial nor complaint. There had been times when she wondered if she had caused greater trouble for him than she knew. Though she could find out nothing that supported her feeling, she seemed to sense that something was kept hidden from her. Perhaps something that affected Timothy so adversely it added to his determination to keep her at arm's length.

Tonight, for a very little while, she had been allowed to think he cared for her as he always had. Surely she had not dreamed that he had called her *My dearest girl*. . . ? But only moments later he had taken care to show her that all he had for her was leftover kindness from the earlier days. Perhaps she should have accepted Justin Prescott's proposal if only to put herself into a different orbit. She summoned back the angry pride. In future she would keep her distance from Timothy, let him see she had learned her lesson, that he meant as little to her as she meant to him.

With something between a sob and a sigh, she began to look for hairpins.

CHAPTER NINE

A MONTH LATER Timothy was again at Danesfield on his firm's business. As before, when it was finished, Nick invited him to stay for lunch and this time he accepted. It was time, he felt, to let the past slide into oblivion; time to allow old custom to fill in the breaches made in friendship.

Meals were punctual in this well-run household. Elise had come to join the two men and with only two or three minutes before the gong summoning them to table might be expected to sound, they were standing in the centre of the drawing-room, with nearly empty glasses of sherry in their hands. Aware of Timothy's presence, Rebecca had delayed her appearance until the last moment, praying he would go. He had not, and unable to defer her appearance any longer, she came in now. She greeted Timothy with brief and distant courtesy, declined the sherry her father offered her, and could find nothing to contribute to the conversation.

Conscious of the slight awkwardness introduced by his daughter's silence, Nick tried to overcome it by recalling the magnificent bouquet of flowers – the best Ambershaws' gardens could provide – received by her the previous day and teasing her about her latest admirer. Jokingly, he complimented her on her likely elevation to the peerage before long and invited Timothy to join with him in congratulating her.

Reluctant to say anything on that particular subject, Timothy forced himself to say lightly, 'She will make a charming countess.'

'Married to a charming buffoon, too.'

Uncertain of the situation and whether that was Nick's genuine opinion of Perry Osmond, or just another tease aimed at Rebecca, Timothy said, 'Oh, no! Perry plays the fool, but he's no fool in fact. He took a first in Classics and is as sensible as any man alive when there is a serious matter in view.' With an effort, he summoned up a smile, looked at Rebecca and said, 'Such as marriage.'

Her father's choice of subject for raillery was particularly unfortunate. In the past four weeks Rebecca had had ample time in which to brood over Timothy's determination to end their old relationship; four weeks in which to nurse her anger and forget her resolve to prove to him her indifference. Staring back at him, she felt a swelling tide of frustration and resentment gathering force in her at his dull-wittedness. To find him ready – eager even – to thrust her into the arms of another man when she loved him so dearly was to add insult to injury . . . and that made worse by the fact that at this moment he was looking at her and smiling. The tide reached flood, demanded outlet: her eyes grey slits of fury, she struck him across the face. It was a hard blow, falling on cheek and mouth and the ring she wore cut his lower lip, drawing blood.

Shock held them all motionless for several moments: even Becca. She stood in appalled wonder at having done such a thing. The mark of her hand was already showing against the sudden whiteness of Timothy's face, yet he neither lifted his own hand to it, nor appeared to give it notice of any kind. But Nick had seen, for the briefest moment, the look that blazed in the green eyes and every muscle in his body had tensed in readiness to defend his daughter. The look had vanished too quickly for the older man even to be sure of what he had seen.

Breaking the spell that held them, Timothy turned to Nick and Elise and said evenly, 'Forgive me, it has occurred to me I was wrong to accept your kind invitation to lunch. I have just recollected that I need to look up several points of law before meeting the client who is coming to consult me early this afternoon. Quite stupid of me to be so forgetful, but I must not be found to be wanting in information. Will you excuse me?'

Grateful for the young man's good sense and good manners, Nick made no attempt to persuade him to remain. Accepting the excuse, he sent a message to the stables for Mr Ryland's horse to be brought to the door and watched approvingly while Timothy said his goodbyes to his wife and daughter in his usual easy way. Rebecca stood throughout as deaf, blind and motionless as Lot's wife after she had looked back at the destruction of the cities of the plain.

Accompanying the young lawyer out of the house, Nick saw him mounted before saying quietly, 'I don't know what the trouble is between you and Becca, but I'm sorry for it, Timothy.' He gave the horse a valedictory pat and stood away.

Timothy did not look back. Swift and wrathful then, Nick re-entered the house, intent on demanding an explanation from his carefully brought up and usually well-behaved daughter. She was not where he had left her.

He looked at Elise. 'Escaped to her room, I suppose?'

She nodded.

'Why did she do it? In Heaven's name, Elise, tell me *why*?'

Shaken by her own action, Rebecca stood in her bedroom as though lost. She did not wonder *why* she had done what she had, but *how* she could have allowed herself to do it. The impulse, bursting up from some deep core of combined anger and unhappiness, had been unstoppable. It was against everything she had ever been taught, but given all the time in the world to consider, she doubted she could have prevented herself expressing in the way she had her thwarted love and longing, her bitterness for the terrors and disappointments that had lain in wait for her once her schooldays had ended. But if Timothy had continued to care for her as once he had, little of the rest would matter.

Timothy's management of the affairs Rupert Lasseter had put in his hands had more than satisfied that exacting gentleman and brought about consultations regarding the transference of other concerns into those same competent hands. The meetings had taken place at Elswick Manor in the course of which he had met Mrs Lasseter and drawn the giggling interest of the 12-year-old twin daughters of the family. Impressed by the young man's appearance and manners, Mrs Lasseter proposed using them for own her purposes. Consequently, when drawing up a guest list for her next party, his name featured among the rest.

Certain that the Mariotts would be among the guests, Timothy was reluctant to accept the invitation he subsequently received, but recognizing that the Lasseter account was too important for him to risk giving offence, he did as he felt he must and accepted it.

He was right in supposing that the Mariotts would be there and so had been prepared to see them. Rebecca had not been prepared to see *him* and was dismayed when she did. She had offered her parents neither reason nor excuse for the blow she had given Timothy when he last came to Danesfield and it remained a matter of battled displeasure between them. Her mother had lectured her on the vulgarity of her action with a severity that she would not easily forget, but it was her father's cold anger that lingered unpleasantly in her consciousness.

Elise saw Timothy in the same moment as her daughter and said sternly, 'Timothy is here, as I am sure you have noticed. I hope you mean to behave yourself as you should towards him. If there is any doubt of it, say so now and we will make an excuse and leave. Neither your father nor I will endure another exhibition such as you made of yourself when you were last in his company.'

In a stifled voice, Rebecca said, 'Nothing like that will happen again, Mama, I promise.'

'If opportunity offers then, I suggest you apologize to him. He, you may be sure, will accept it with courtesy. If you are able to offer him the explanation you have withheld from your father and from me, he may even be able to forgive you in fact as well as in civility.'

The idea of attempting even the simplest apology made Rebecca half sick with apprehension. Her emotions where Timothy was concerned were tangled beyond all unravelling. As it happened, she was given no opportunity to attempt apology or explanation: Timothy did not approach her at any time during the evening and proved singularly elusive when she tried to approach *him*. He did not neglect to speak to her parents, but the only times she saw him with them was when she was locked into a dance with no chance of escape from it.

The Lasseters had provided as royally as ever for their guests. There were entertainments and dancing throughout the evening and a superb supper in a flower-decked room with small, charming gifts for everyone present. With so much to please the mood of the evening was generally euphoric, but Rebecca longed only for the time to go home.

The Osmonds did not figure among the Lasseters' acquaintance so neither Perry nor Helena was there. Rebecca wished they were. She did not lack partners, but the presence of the brother and sister would have gone some way to compensating for the distance that Timothy so resolutely maintained between them. In a muddle of resentment and relief, she was a disappointing partner; those who sought her out finding her preoccupied and silent. Conscious of it, she tried to rouse herself to sparkle, but with little success.

To be out of favour with so many people was a new experience for Rebecca and a far from pleasurable one. Whenever her gaze fell on Timothy, it seemed to her that he appeared to be positively flaunting his popularity with young and old alike. That to do so was alien to his nature, she knew, but something raw and painful in her demanded that his image in her mind and her opinion of him be diminished, as hers, she was sure, was in *his*.

As the carriage carried them the short distance back to Danesfield, Elise asked Rebecca, 'Did you speak to Timothy?'

'No. He gave me no opportunity. He did not come near me the whole evening and it seemed to me he deliberately made it impossible for me to approach him.'

'Are you surprised?'

'I suppose not,' Rebecca said reluctantly. 'But we shall have to meet again sometime. It would have been as well to have got it over and done with.'

'As well for *you* perhaps. But Timothy is the injured party and may not see it as you do.'

Altogether, Rebecca thought, it had been a wretched evening.

The first week of August was hot and sunny, but the heat continued to build and in the second week became oppressive. Ponds and streams began to dry, the sky was leached of colour except for coppery tinges in the distance. Thunder growled like an ill-tempered dog that threatened but was not sufficiently awake to take action. The night skies were restless with the flickering of sheet lightning.

Immured in the airless, mind-sapping stuffiness of his small office, Timothy found it difficult to concentrate on the more complicated documents that came his way. Every window in the building was open but no relief from outside came in through them. The motionless air trapped in the narrow streets of the area lost little warmth at night and simply gathered more heat to itself the next day.

When the temperature reached 95°, it was felt no more could be borne and as if in agreement, at midday the heavens darkened to near night-time and the land held its breath in anticipation. The first blinding blast of light coincided with a crack of thunder so violent that it might have been the sound of the world splitting in two. For several seconds this forceful duet was repeated and repeated as though light and sound fought for mastery. It was ended by a rumble so lengthy it seemed it would never end. When it did, the silence that followed was profound though it lasted only a few minutes before the rain came. This fell, not as drops, but in a solid, roaring weight of water that drove a number of those unfortunate enough to be caught in the open to their knees. Ten minutes later, as suddenly as it began, that, too, stopped.

Humanity, expecting some relief, was given very little: buildings steamed and humidity rose sharply. Discomfort piled on discomfort. And then, like an orchestral encore, the storm began again. Thunder cracked and rumbled, lightning made a white, continuous dazzle and rain flooded down, stopped as though drawing breath and then began again. The streets were awash. Church bells rang though the notes were only audible in the heavens' quieter moments. Altogether, it was enough to confirm the nervous in a belief that the end of the world had come . . . a belief strengthened when the intermittent storm showed no abatement through the next forty-eight hours.

The third day was Sunday and only then did the stormbursts begin to draw apart and lessen their fury. Congregations overflowed the churches. In the afternoon, Timothy hired a horse from the livery-stables, a familiar animal named Felix, and headed out of Chichester's flooded, debris-littered streets towards Elswick. Little and contradictory news from the coastal villages had filtered into the city. That there had been wild seas to add to their troubles Timothy did not doubt; tales of the quantity of flotsam thrown up on the shoreline gathered detail in the telling. Reports abounded of boats having been wrecked that had been thought to be drawn up to points well beyond harm's way. More worrying was the number of ships thought to be at sea when the storms started and not yet known to have returned to any port.

The five miles to Elswick was accomplished slowly and with difficulty. His mount, patient though he was, had been without exercise for several days and was in two minds, wanting to stretch his legs on one hand but jibbing nervously at the occasional last mutterings of thunder, the intermittent flare of lightning and spiteful downpours on the other. There were obstacles too, that compelled detours or which needed careful negotiation, making it an uncomfortable and tedious journey.

Reliable news was what Timothy wanted first. Though the probability was that he would meet Rebecca at Danesfield, he chose to go there rather than to either Andy or Giles's homes. He wanted no squabble with either brother, supposing they were not among those caught at sea. He accepted that he might meet Rebecca. Better that it should happen in the presence of one, or both, of her parents than otherwise.

He had hoped Nick might be at home, but he was out inspecting the latest damage on the estate and he was shown into the small room looking north-easterly over the fields. It had the best light for the embroidery with which both Elise and Rebecca were engaged; Rebecca with a tambour in hand and Elise with an embroidery frame before her.

'Mrs Mariott . . . Miss Mariott. . .' He aimed his smile and his bow somewhere between them, but spoke directly to Elise. 'Forgive my breaking in on you like this. Being in dispute with my father, as you know, I do not visit my old home. But I am anxious for news of them all and have come to ask what you can tell me of them.'

Looking troubled, Elise said, 'Only that *The Joyous Lady* was expected to return on the day the storm began but has not done so yet. She is not the only ship awaited. There are three others overdue. We think – hope – they made for shelter before it all began. Andy sailed with Josh this last time, not on his own sloop. Some sort of comfort for your mother, given Josh's seamanship, but a double worry nevertheless. You might find Giles at home. He could probably give you more recent news than can I.'

'Andy and Giles know nothing of what lies between my father and myself and so naturally stand with him where I'm concerned, which is why I have come to you.' His wry smile flickered and vanished.

He was aware of Rebeca's head lifting sharply and that her lips shaped for speech, but a warning look from her mother made her subside, colour flooding up into her cheeks. He wondered what what she had been about to say. Something to sting, he suspected.

'Giles's wife is tied to their own home by the needs of her two little ones, but they spend what time they can with your mother and she and Andy's Jill draw some comfort from one another. Prue is not left to worry alone for too long,' Elise said.

It was all she could tell him and excusing himself from remaining longer, he headed for the village to see what might be gleaned there. The track to Blackthorns lay quiet and empty, only the roof and chimneys of the house to be seen from the lane because of the dip in the land in which it had been built. Two fields beyond, it was a different matter; here it seemed, half the village was gathered. The gate to the field stood wide and he rode through to the edge of the crowd and, dismounting, tethered the horse to the sturdiest hedge sapling he could see. Not that the docile animal was likely to wander far even if left free.

The cause of the excitement was abundantly clear. Two or three hundred yards offshore a lugger was stranded on a sandbank. She had lost her mizzen mast and a quantity of rigging, but was still instantly recognizable to Timothy as *The Joyous Lady*. Most of the crew, equally recognizable to him, stood or sat in a soaked and dispirited group into which wives, parents, children were infiltrating, anxious for the final reassurance of being able to touch the one they sought. How the men had been brought to shore was being demonstrated by the number of men – among them Giles – hauling on the double rope that stretched out through the sea to the stranded ship.

The crowd was too engrossed with watching the rescue to notice Timothy and few among those who happened to glance his way recognized him. He chose a youngster he could not himself identify and asked how many more there were to be brought to land.

'Only the two they're bringing in now, the captain and his son. The two together because the captain was killed or injured when the mast came down.' With no knowledge of who it was he was speaking to, the youngster spoke blithely, happy to pass on knowledge to a stranger and a city man to judge by his appearance. 'It's hard going against the sea that's running and the tide's on the turn to make it worse,' he added instructively, with no depth of concern, not having anyone of his own among the crew.

Timothy watched in the frustration of uselessness. There was nothing he could do. Not even the token gesture of adding his weight to that of the other men: the rope was manned to the last inch by willing helpers. It seemed an age before a small cheer greeted the first glimpse of a head lifted above the surging waters close to shore. In a moment, Giles abandoned his position on the pulley-rope and having got someone to secure a rope round his waist, waded into the seethe of waters to help in dragging Josh and Andy over the lip of the land.

Andy sat coughing and retching up the salt water that had forced a way down his throat, but Josh lay ominously still and unaware of anything.

For a minute or two Timothy watched Giles's ineffectual efforts to wring some sign of life from Josh before crossing to them.

'Is he alive?' he asked.

'There's a pulse. He's breathing,' Giles answered, before he realized who had asked the question.

Through the babble in the field, Timothy caught it then, Josh's faint, snoring inhalation. As he watched, blood from a head wound that had been staunched by the sea, began to seep out again to colour his hair and the water running from it.

Now, too, Giles realized who it was had spoken to him. 'What are *you* doing here?' he demanded, hostility bristling through every word.

'Much the same as you, except I arrived too late to be useful. Now I can be. I have a quiet horse. If we can get Father across his back, it will be the best and quickest way to get him home to his bed and to mother's care. Andy's in no case to do much more than get himself home.'

Giles considered the suggestion, his desire to reject it obvious, but was forced in the end to acknowledge the sense of it and to nod acceptance.

Timothy collected Felix, led him to where his father lay and stripped off the saddle. Accosting the nearest youngster, he offered him sixpence to carry the saddle to Blackthorns, an offer joyfully accepted. It was clear that Andy, exhausted by the burdened journey he had made through rough water, was having difficulty finding the strength needed to match Giles's in hoisting Josh upright, but when Timothy stepped forward to help, Giles snarled, 'Stand away! Andy and I and our friends can do all he needs.' His eyes were savage with worry and anger. 'If severance from the family is what you want – you've got it: we can do without you.'

Timothy stood back; said nothing. In his mind he heard an echo of Andy saying, . . . *you're no brother of mine*. Heard his own bitter words to his father, *I shall not willingly enter your house again*. . . . And step by step the wholly unwanted separation from his family had begun. What was it Nick had said? *Consequences wait like sharks beneath the ocean's surface*. . . . Even in trying to distance himself from Becca, he had succeeded chiefly in alienating her.

As Giles had said, any of their friends and neighbours who were not otherwise engaged were willing to help and Timothy stood holding Felix in place until, with rough determination, Josh was laid safely across the animal's back. Pressure on his stomach brought on a brief, choking spell of coughing until he vomited up some of the water he had taken in.

Both Josh and Andy were without their heavy sea-boots, sensibly abandoned for the watery ship to shore journey. With his brothers holding Josh steady on either side, and trailed by the saddle-bearer, Timothy led Felix at a slow pace along the field path to Blackthorns, allowing Andy, bootless as he was, to walk on grass rather than the grit of the road.

The news regarding *The Joyous Lady* had reached Prue by the time they arrived at Blackthorns. She had the door of the cottage open and hurried out to them as soon as they reached the stable. She hovered anxiously until assured that Josh was alive, watched him lifted from the horse's back, then slipped away back to the house to prepare for his reception.

His young porter paid off, Timothy slapped the saddle back on to Felix as soon as there was space for it. Giles stood nearest him, and to him Timothy said, 'You'll need help if you plan to get him upstairs to his bed.'

Giles's blue eyes glared hostilely at Timothy. 'I told you, we can manage without you. There's still enough of us in the family to do what's needed. The women will help.'

Useless to argue with Giles, Timothy knew. He turned to buckle the saddle into place and adjust the girth. Andy and Giles were already lumbering into the house with their awkward burden in a makeshift sling of horse blankets, finding it heavy even for them.

As he had hoped, his mother came to the door to look for him. He went to kiss her cheek and say encouragingly, 'Don't worry yourself to death, Mother. Let us see what the doctor has to say. I'll go and find one now. Who do you favour these days?'

'Doctor Haines at Selsey. He's the nearest – if he'll come.'

'If I find him, he'll come, don't fret. Where does he live?'

'His house is this end of the village. Anyone will tell you.'

He swung himself into the saddle. 'I'll be as quick as I can. It was Andy, by the way, who brought Father to shore. He must have had a difficult job keeping an unconscious man from drowning with the seas still running high and heavy. Giles will tell you the rest. But see Andy gets out of his wet clothes and a good drink down him.' His smile twisted. '*Me* instructing *you*!' Wheeling Felix around, he headed for the road.

Less than an hour later, he and the doctor rode in together. Timothy saw the man to door of the house and into his mother's hands before going to stable the grey mare.

When Prue next looked for her youngest son, there was no one there.

CHAPTER TEN

THE DOOR OF his living-room opening lifted Timothy's attention from the book he was reading. A glance at the clock showed it to be a few minutes past nine. An unexpected visitor at this time of the evening was unusual. Setting down his book, he rose to his feet as Giles stepped into the room and stood looking at him with no kindly expression. Timothy waited.

'I'm here,' Giles told him, on a note somewhere between belligerence and contempt, 'to tell you Ma wants to see you. You, of course, are all anxiety to know how your father's doing.' The contempt increased. 'Two days gone by, Timothy, and not a word of enquiry, dammit!'

'That's a different tune from the last I heard you sing. Would I have been given an answer to any enquiry I made?' Timothy felt no inclination to explain that, bypassing his brothers, he had provided himself with a dependable line of information.

Having no ready answer to that, Giles gave it none. 'Well, I'm telling you now; Pa's concussed, but his skull's not broken. He sleeps a deal of the time and isn't always sensible when he's awake, but the doctor says that'll improve as time passes. But Ma's in a worry just the same and what matters is that she wants to see you. So come to Blackthorns Sunday. Fail, and I'll come and haul you in.'

'If Mother wants to see me, I'll be there.'

'That's it then.' Giles nodded, but remained standing where he was, turning something over in his mind. Again,Timothy waited.

'You were a good enough little nipper,' Giles said at last. 'Must have been that fancy school twisted you. Andy says you blame Pa for the split between you. For some reason, Pa has never said anything about it one way or another. What's plain is, whatever it was, it doesn't sit easy with him. But *you* – you take it easy enough! As though it makes no matter to you. Like the family means nothing to you, these days.'

'How would you know?'

'If it mattered, you'd have done something by now to put things right?'

' "*Even God cannot change the past—*" '

'Oh, if you're coming the clever man over me, I'm off?' He turned to the door, snatched it open and flung back over his shoulder, 'Blackthorns. Sunday. Be there! *Or by that same God, I'll see you rue it*!'

Two hours past noon on Sunday, Timothy rode out to Elswick. He passed Danesfield and turned in where the familiar track crossed Danesfield land to Blackthorns. Dismounting, he tied the horse to a ring in the stable wall before knocking on the door of the house. He had not been aware of any sound coming from within, but somehow a silence seemed to deepen about the place, as though the house itself was listening. The door opened and his mother stood framed within the doorway, Giles behind her looking smug.

'*Timothy*! 'His mother was pleased. 'Come in.'

He leaned to kiss her cheek and smile reassuringly at her. 'No, Mama. Would you oblige me and come out? We can find somewhere to sit in the sun and talk.'

'You do what Ma wants. No reason why she should do want *you* want.' That was Giles in authoritative mood.

Timothy looked at him. 'You're master in your own house, I don't doubt, Giles,' he said, 'but that house is not Blackthorns. Mother will decide for herself'

The belligerency in Giles's expression increased. It was obvious he was poised to launch himself into verbal and possibly physical combat and Prue said sharply, 'Enough! I have sufficient worries with your father in a bad way without you two falling into a dispute on the doorstep.'

Giles subsided but not without having the last word. 'Look to yourself little brother. I'll have my due out of you when I'm ready.'

Prue stepped out on to the path, saying crossly, 'One more word out of you, Giles, and it is *I* who will have my due out of *you*. Shut the door and go back to the others.' She waited until the door was closed then turned to her youngest son, saying, 'As for you – the rift between you and Josh is upsetting everyone . . . making things difficult for us all.'

'You know what caused the rift.'

'Yes. And I also know that only *you* can bridge it.'

Timothy let that pass without remark, but asked, 'How is he? Is there any improvement?'

'He's mending, thank God. But the doctor tells us it will take time for full recovery. He sleeps a lot and when he wakes his mind is often on things far back in the past. He remembers little yet of anything recent. Sometimes he wonders where you are as though he has forgotten you have left home.'

They had turned towards the sea and were strolling down through the small orchard with its trees stunted by fierce salt winds yet still managing to be productive if only in a small way. At the low boundary hedge they halted as though by consent, standing looking out across the bridle-path that edged the land to the heaving water still discoloured by churned up sand and silt, but showing far less of its tumultuous power to destroy than it had.

'How did they come to be stranded?'

'Andy says the storm that caught them came like a spiteful afterclap when the worst seemed to be over. They had seen it gathering behind them, but were so near home Josh decided to try and outrun it. It came on them faster than they had thought possible and hit them like the fist of God, Andy says. The mizzen-mast came down with its rigging and some part of it hit Josh and laid him flat. Andy took over, of course, but there was nothing they could do but keep on and hope to make harbour. The sooner the better for Josh's sake. They seemed to be in luck when they saw how close to home they were. But you know what the undercurrents are like from the Bill round to Pagham and how the sea-bed shifts and changes. Driven as they were, they ended up on a new sandbank.'

'Is *The Joyous Lady* lost?'

'No. Damaged, but not beyond repair. Everyone expected the sea would take her, but somehow she clung to the sandbank and suffered the pounding the waves gave her. On the next high tide, she was towed off, brought to shelter as close to shore as is safe and made fast. Thank God for good neighbours and good seamen! We even had some naval men who went to her help in their sloop.'

The sun filtered down through the trees, dappling the grass, its touch very different from a short time ago when it had blasted heat at them as though the doors of hell had suddenly been flung wide.

'Timothy!' Prue called his wandering attention back to her on a note different from the one she had used so far. 'Josh has you on his mind. In his occasional lucid moments, it frets him that you brought him home that day. He's puzzled by it.'

'He's confused, Mother. It was not I who brought him home, I merely lent the horse that carried him here. Andy and Giles did everything else. Andy got him safely through the sea to the shore, unconscious though he was, and that could have been no easy task. He and Giles together hoisted him over the horse's back and held him there. Giles was ready to go for my throat if I laid a finger on him to help. I didn't think Father gained consciousness once during the journey to know *who* had charge of him.'

'Nevertheless, he seems convinced you played a part in his rescue and, as I said, it puzzles him.'

'He dreamed it. Before long he'll probably be thinking I tried to drown him.'

'Why should he think that?' She frowned at him. 'You're too bitter, Son. You go too far and it doesn't become you.'

The sharp gleam of deep anger came into Timothy's eyes. 'Do I? Father found it easy enough to believe me capable of getting the schoolgirl daughter of his closest friend with child. And she as near to being a sister as she could be without there being a blood link! Patricide can only seem to him a short step further.' He made a derisive sound in his throat. 'What did I ever do to make him think so well of me?'

'I know you find it hard to forgive him, but any other man could have made the mistake he did.'

'He isn't any other man: he's my father!'

'He's human. Why should *he*, any more than Nick, have reason to doubt what Becca said?'

'Because he's Josh. Because he is – *was* – my lodestar. Mother, I can't help it – it's how I *feel*! I can't shrug it aside, forgive and forget. I loved, admired, idolized him. But by his own showing, he holds me worthless. I disgust him – he told me so.'

'That was when he thought you had given him cause.'

'And how readily he believed it, being already disposed to a low opinion of me.'

'You're wrong. But what is the use of my telling you that? I'll tell you instead that you may have admired and idolized him, but you could not have loved him. Love doesn't let go so easily.'

'Love seeks . . . needs . . . begs return.' He turned her to face him. And she saw a strain and a tension in him she had not seen before. This was the son who always kept dogged control of himself: a control that to her fond eye had its own eloquence though never before had she guessed at the full depth of what lay behind it.

'My experience is not great,' he said, 'but what I have seen of men and their sons tells me that every man expects to see something of himself in his son. A total want of resemblance of *some* kind – character, looks, skill, *something* – seems to me more than half the cause of their dissensions. When Josh looks at Andy or Giles he sees a mirror image of himself. What does he see when he looks at me? Nothing at all of himself! Not looks, colouring, height, breadth, strength, seamanship, nor fellowship of thinking. All he sees is *the runt of the family*, as Andy told me recently when he generously restrained himself from pummelling me into telling him what he wanted to know. A poor thing! Lacking brawn and having to rely on brain. You've said it makes no difference, but I say it does.'

Prue drew a deep breath. Her green eyes narrowed and glittered with anger, emphasizing the resemblance between them. 'Follow that line of thought to its end, my son, and you'll be asking me, *Mother, am I your husband's child*?' Her look scorched him. 'So, you think me a whore, do you! Let me now ask *you* a question: *whose bastard do you choose to think yourself*?'

Timothy was shaken, as much by her vehemence as by her words. 'Mother, *no*! Such a thought never crossed my mind. *Could not*! If I made it sound so, I do most humbly beg your pardon.'

'And no doubt you expect easy forgiveness from me for a transgression equal to any of your father's against you. You won't get it! Take yourself away. You deserve every stripe Josh gave you. It is Josh and I who need pity for having produced you.'

She turned from him and would have hurried back to the house, but he gripped her arm and held it with bruising strength. 'Don't go! I implore you, don't go!'

There was a passion of entreaty in his voice Prue had never heard from him before. It shocked her into immobility.

He shifted his grip to her hand and carried it briefly to his lips. Words tumbling from him, he said, 'I did not intend to imply . . . indeed, I did not! I cannot . . . *cannot* . . . lose your kindness, too. It's all I have left. I wish to God I'd been bred to the sea like the other two. On my knees if you will, to you as to no one else in this world, I beg your forgiveness.'

Shocked again, Prue looked at the down-bent dark red-brown head. Because he always appeared so much his own man, so self-sufficient, with everything firmly under control of that same well-filled head, perhaps too much had been taken for granted about this youngest son. Had she and Josh been a little too ready to smooth his path to material success and in doing so, overlooked that he was being deprived in other areas? Always different, the odd child out, but now, in these moments of rare revelation, showing such an unguessed-at depth of raw feeling, such a sense of isolation, she was lost in her own feelings of guilt and hurt. He looked up at her, released her hand and straightened. The moment of weakness was past: already, she saw, he was drawing the shield of steely control back into place.

'You must think me a fool and childish with it. My troubles I bring on myself, don't I?' He gave her a wry, heart-wrenching smile. 'Am I cast off?'

With difficulty holding her own emotions in check, Prue shook her head. 'No. Never that. Let off with a warning, let us say. You, I hope, will find it easier to forgive as you grow older and discover how vulnerable we all are. But Timothy, the trouble between you and your father hurts *me* . . .'

'I have not your quality, Mother. I cannot match your

generosity. I loved my father, but I cannot forgive him. *Because* I loved my father, I cannot forgive him.'

Loved, admired, idolized, he had said. And always from the age of ten separated by distance and circumstances while his brothers remained close to the idol. One did not realize—

She said sadly, 'And what of me, Timothy? I stand between you and Josh, loving you equally, though differently. When one inflicts pain on the other, I feel it as much – perhaps *more* – than either of you. If you have any love for *me*, keep it in mind!'

CHAPTER ELEVEN

TOWARDS THE END of the first week of September, the Osmond family returned from a two-month stay in their summer place on the Devon coast A few days later Nick handed a note across the breakfast table to Elise and said, 'It appears we are indebted to our daughter for further acquaintance with the Earl and Countess of Ambershaw. With her, we are invited to a private performance of *Othello* at Ambershaws.'

Having read the invitation, Elise looked back at him to say quirkily, 'Let me remind you that Becca owes her introduction to the Osmonds to Timothy who knew the son and heir, Perry Osmond, in their Oxford days. I'm told Lord Osmond made a point of seeking him out in order to renew the acquaintance after the Charlton-Jarrad case brought the name to his attention.' She handed back the invitation. 'I imagine we are to go?'

'Oh, certainly. Would Rebecca ever forgive me if I declined the invitation?' Nick reached for the marmalade and said thoughtfully, 'Timothy progresses by leaps and bounds, doesn't he? It must seem as strange to Josh's nest of seahawks to hatch out an eagle in their midst as it is for small birds to find themselves saddled with a cuckoo.'

'I am not sure that Becca will welcome the invitation. And if she does, it may not be for Perry Osmond's sake. In fact, I am not at all sure of what her state of mind is where either Perry or Timothy is concerned. She does not confide as easily as once she did. I think we should tread warily there, Nick.'

'Don't tell me our daughter has social aspirations she hopes to fulfil by her own efforts without the tie of a husband? How long does she think her social elevation would last if she turns down the future Earl of Ambershaw? *My* standing will not keep her at that level.'

Elise's attention was arrested. 'Do you think Lord Osmond has serious intentions where Becca is concerned?'

Nick shrugged. 'Who can tell? It is what Ambershaw might say to such a proposition that is likely to have most importance, I should think. But what makes you suspect Becca reluctant to accept the invitation?'

'Timothy. He is sure to be there.'

Nick's expression darkened. 'Then she had better watch her step. I have not forgiven her for her behaviour when last she saw him here. Timothy, of all people! No matter what may lie between them as man and woman, when she was in dire need, he met that need without hesitation and paid for doing it. Through me; through Josh. And dearly where Josh is concerned. As Josh is now paying for the mistake he made because of it. Mischief all set afoot by Rebecca's lie.'

'She hasn't been told what happened between Josh and Timothy, Nick. And she was a child when it happened. A shocked and frightened child with not even her mother at hand to turn to. That has to be remembered.'

'Well, I think it past time she learned the trouble she caused among good friends she had no right to involve. She's older by eighteen months or more, and should have begun carrying her own responsibilities, or at least some of them. She's half the woman her mother was at her age.'

'She's a different person. Has a different temperament.'

He was silent a moment or two and then with a wry smile,

conceded, 'Yes. As different from you as I was from my father. I should remember and show more understanding, should I not?' He pushed back his chair and stood up. 'Will you excuse me, my dear – I have Pettigrew waiting for me.' He did not move away from the table immediately, however, but stood gripping the top rail of his chair, lost in frowning thought again until, as though speaking his last thought aloud, he said, 'Am I too harsh with the girl? Have I made her afraid of me?'

Seeming to expect no answer to his questions, he turned to the door, at which Elise sprang up and caught at his ann. 'Nick, don't say anything to her at present, please. Promise me! There's a right time and a wrong time for Becca to know all that her involving Timothy did. Believe me, *now* is not the time.'

He turned back. 'No, I won't do that, but for *your* sake, not hers. I'm out of patience with her.'

'Don't judge her too harshly. Remember she had a terrible shock when she was barely out of childhood, and leaving that behind isn't done in a moment. As I said, I don't understand the present situation between Becca, Lord Osmond and Timothy. I suspect Becca doesn't either.'

'*That* I can well believe!'

'Try to be patient, Nick,' she coaxed. 'I think we need to be kind.'

'Whenever are you not so? It is I who am the impatient ogre!' He stood looking at her, his dark gaze warming and an odd little smile slowly softening the severe line of his mouth. 'Though there was an occasion when you lost patience with me, I remember. I wanted to kiss you, and you knew it. Knew that I drew back from it because I was annoyed at finding I had fallen in love with you when I wanted to continue to disapprove of you. You told me very briskly at the time that the heart is sometimes wiser than the head.'

Responsive as always to his mood, she sparkled back at him.

'And disapprove of me you did – then and afterwards! You told me in return that I was the biggest busybody on earth, deserving of any unpleasant thing that happened to me. My goodness, how many years ago was that?'

'Twenty-two at least. Even if I was slow to give it recognition, I loved you then as much as any man could love any woman and I love you not one grain the less now.' He bent to drop a kiss on her nose before walking away to the door. There, he again turned back, but briefly this time to say, 'I promise to be both patient and kind where our daughter is concerned. As much, that is, as it lies within my nature to be. Which cannot raise your expectation very high, my darling, but shows me willing.' He gave her the slanting smile that for a moment wiped twenty years from his age and then he was gone.

Rebecca breakfasted early and had left the table before her parents came to it. A note from Lady Helena came to her by the same post as her parents' invitation. In her bedroom, she read it again. It told her she must be sure to keep Tuesday 17th of the month free of all other engagements and that Mr and Mrs Mariott were to receive a formal invitation from her parents which she hoped they would accept. The day was to be a gala occasion with music and a buffet supper to be served following the performance. Perry, Helena had added, was planning to invite Timothy and to drop a word in Mr Diment's ear to ensure his junior partner's early release to attend. All of which meant to Rebecca that she would be in close company with Timothy, but under difficult circumstances in which to fulfil any hope she might have for bringing about a reconciliation between them. Perry and Helena, she was fairly certain, had their own designs for the occasion where she and Timothy were concerned.

She wished that she might reply to the note regretting her inability to accept the invitation because of an unalterable prior engagement but because her parents had been invited choice was denied her. And with all the difficulties she foresaw in meeting Timothy, underneath was an irrational longing just to be where he was.

As the weeks had passed the enormity of what she had done in striking him, had loomed larger and larger in her mind. He had been her parents' guest, not hers, which added to the outrage as they must see it. It seemed to her impossible to explain to them the many emotions that had come together to exert such pressure that she had forgotten every rule of her breeding and allowed herself to display what they must regard as a total want of delicacy. As for Timothy himself – what inference he had drawn from the blow she could not imagine. That it had set him at an even greater distance from her, he had made clear and she could see no way of lessening it.

Fortune smiled on Ambershaws' gala day. It fell in a week of fine weather, exceptionally warm for the time of the year.

As Rebecca expected, Lady Helena had attached herself to Timothy before the Mariotts' arrival and Perry appeared to have been waiting only for Rebecca to come. She could not even seek refuge with her parents because the Earl and Countess drew them into their own group with a particularity that made it impossible to do anything else but accept that she was marked out as Perry's guest.

Both Nick and Elise were surprised by the distinguishing notice they received from their host and hostess, even though they supposed that they were chiefly received as the parents of a friend of the earl's son and heir. That it went beyond that Nick soon learned when, walking alone with the earl, his lordship said, 'You have a charming and very beautiful daughter, Mr Mariott. Perry is very much taken with her.'

'I have wondered if that is a matter of concern to you,' Nick said forthrightly.

'No. I was allowed to make my own choice of wife and have been very happy in that choice. Within reason, I think it only fair my son should have the same privilege. Fortunately, Perry has a well-developed sense of responsibility and has already spoken of the matter to me. I told him what I have told you, adding only that there must be no objection to the match on your side. Not everyone regards a titled bridegroom for their daughter as an entire blessing.' He laughed drily. 'Though I must say, most do.'

'With or without the title, my wife and I would welcome Perry as a husband for Rebecca. But—'

'Ah. So not completely plain sailing?'

'No. I have no certainty where Rebecca's feelings for Perry are concerned, but if Perry has marriage in mind, there is something both he and you are entitled to know before the matter goes any further. I prefer to tell you what it is and to allow you to decide how much difference it makes and – if you you so resolve – to tell Perry.' Rushing the last fence, he said, 'Through no fault worse than innocence and ignorance, my daughter is not a virgin.'

'I see.' The tone was not encouraging.

'What I am about to tell you is the truth. Whether or not you believe me is for you to decide. A month after Rebecca left the schoolroom, we gave a coming-out ball for her. The weather was pleasantly warm. There was dancing both in the house and on the lawns. Some elderly friends of ours brought with them a nephew, or great-nephew, who was their guest at the time; a sophisticated man of thirty, married and living in London. He paid Becca a great deal of attention, persuaded her to show him the gazebo and there produced champagne and glasses from his pockets and proceeded to make her drunk. Naïve, inexperienced, she had no idea of what he was about. When she was sufficiently confused and helpless, he raped her. By it, she conceived a child. At the time her old nurse discovered it, my wife was away in France and her return, unfortunately, was for various reasons, twice delayed. When Rebecca was four months into term with the child, her nurse insisted that I was told. No doubt I handled it clumsily. Panic-stricken at my insistence that the man be made to marry her and knowing it was impossible, Rebecca claimed her childhood friend, Timothy Ryland, was the father. Timothy, her champion since she was a child of three, rose to the occasion and agreed to marry her. Ironically, her mother came back to us in the evening of the next day. Becca was in the garden. Hearing the sounds of her mother's arrival and hurrying to meet her, she tripped at the top of some awkward stone steps in the garden and fell their length. It was not known she was there and she was not found for some time. She lost the baby and was ill for some weeks after. There, you have it.'

With a pride as icy as any the earl himself might show, he added, 'Whether or not you believe me, I leave to you. Whatever conclusion you come to, I and my family will accept without complaint. I do not know what Rebecca's feelings are for Perry, but if they are such that she suffers disappointment, she will accept it with dignity. The one thing before which I turn craven is having to be the one to repeat the story to a young man you say is in love with her. I leave you in your wisdom to do that, my lord.'

Ambershaw's gaze had held Nick's throughout and after only a short pause, he said, 'I believe what you have told me, Mr Mariott, and thank you for your honesty. It could not have been easy. Until I have spoken to my son I cannot tell you what the outcome will be. We must wait and see.'

A temporary stage had been erected in the ballroom. The play was well produced, well acted. When it was over, with a degree of haste, Lady Helena steered Timothy out of a side-door into the garden.

'Everyone will be going into supper now, but you must wait. I promise you won't starve and that you will have your share of the best.' She laughed up at him and steered him rapidly along the paths until they came to a narrow wrought-iron gate that gave on to a path between shrubs in need of trimming.

'No one will come here,' Helena said, as Timothy closed the gate behind them. 'It is known as the children's garden. The neglected look at the entrance is deliberate, a disincentive to uninvited visitors. It saves bothering with keys that can never be found when one wants them. Beyond the first bend which, as you see is just ahead, we shall find the gardens kept as tidily as elsewhere.'

She led the way forward on a path with side tracks leading into shrubberies just right for games of hide-and-seek, not stopping until they came to an open area set about with various pieces of equipment for children's amusement. All were old and worn but maintained in good repair. Under a well-grown beech tree from one sturdy branch of which hung a swing, she halted. Waving an inclusive hand, she offered him a choice of the rest, saying, 'Sit wherever you choose as long as we can see each other while we talk. I claim the swing because it was always my favourite.' She seated herself as she spoke, her lilac-coloured skirts billowing around her before sinking into graceful folds.

She was looking her best, Timothy thought, with an appreciative smile. Devon sunshine had put a hint of gold on her skin and burnished her nut-brown hair. Always handsome, the extra gloss of healthy well-being took her close to beauty.

He had remained standing and she flashed him a sparkling glance. 'I think what was always Nurse's chair just to your right will accord best with your dignity, besides providing most comfort.' With a small push of an elegantly shod foot against the trimmed turf she set the swing in gentle motion.

'I suppose,' she said, not looking at him once he had seated himself, 'while Perry and I were frolicking on Devon's golden sands or riding the wide and lonely moorlands, you were working your brain to the bone – if that's what lawyers do.'

Despite her light and careless tone, some instinct warned him that she had brought him here for a purpose. Being unable to guess what it might be, he answered her as lightly as she had chosen to speak. 'Since I like to eat, I've certainly been grateful for what work I've had while you were away. Did you enjoy your holiday?'

'My life is all holiday. *Plus ça change, plus c'est la même chose.*' For a moment she studied the richly hued dapples with which the last of the sunlight, falling through the leaves of the beech tree, stippled her skirt as she swung to and fro. And then, abruptly, she asked, 'Did you miss us?'

'I did.'

'You said that very easily. Not a hint of suffering in it.' She raised her bright hazel gaze from her skirt to look at him. 'Did you miss *me*?'

'I did. My answer was inclusive.' His smile teased her. 'But suppose I said *no, I did not miss you* . . . how was our conversation to progress from that point?'

She smiled a little abstractedly. 'Don't ask questions that are impossible to answer. I admit to fishing. I was hoping to extract a little enthusiasm from you.'

'Lawyers are not supposed to show enthusiasm. They are supposed to be calm, level-headed and wise while their clients do the ranting.'

'What boring lives you lead. And I imagined your life was all cut and thrust with the public cheering on the side-lines. Well, you must have done *something* besides work in the past eight or nine weeks. Have you found a rich widow who will feel privileged to improve your style of life?'

'None who would look at me.'

'Grandmama is a widow and rich. She looked hard enough at you before saying you were a handsome young fellah.'

'Is she looking for a husband? I might consider—'

'Oh Timothy, I wish you would be serious for a while. Forget Grandmama. *I* am the one looking for a husband. A *particular* husband. I'm not a widow, but I am rich. My godfather was a bachelor. He died two years ago and left me his entire, not inconsiderable, fortune.'

'What do I say? Are congratulations appropriate?'

'No. What you should say is, *Helena will you marry me*?'

He laughed. 'Now you're playing Perry's role.'

Frowning, she shook her head. 'Please don't make this any harder for me than it is. I'm not playing the fool. Unmaidenly as it is, I am proposing to you because you won't propose to me.' And then with a valiant attempt to lighten the moment, she added, 'I have authority for it – it's leap year. If you turn me down, remember I have the right to claim a silk gown.'

He dared not abandon the pretence that they were still joking. Lightly, he said, 'I can't afford a silk gown and I can't afford a wife. What am I to do?'

Her gaze shifted to distance and there was a lengthy pause before she said, 'Well, no one could say you jumped at the opportunity! If I must be rejected then I'm glad you did it quietly, rather than decorating it with flim-flam about how *honoured* you are *but*— If you had, I don't think I could forgive you. But if you had, you would not be Timothy.' Then overtaken by her disappointment, her brave smile twisted and she said resentfully, 'Not for Timothy Ryland a titled wife, well-dowered and offering herself almost on her knees.'

He said sharply, 'Helena, don't! Please don't. I feel badly enough as it is. What an unbearably arrogant upstart you must think me!'

'*No*!' She turned her head away from him trying to hide the tears. '*No, I don't! It was a small-minded and unfair thing to say. I apologize.*'

Silence locked around them. The rim of the sun was edging

below the horizon now. Everything within sight was coated with gold; the air itself shimmered with it, but it was the last gleaming of the bright day. In a few minutes all the golden glimmer would be gone and dusk would begin to hang out its blue veils. Timothy sought desperately for a way to counteract the humiliation she must feel, but his mind remained bankrupt of inspiration. And then Helena said fiercely, 'Timothy, say *something*! I am beginning to feel I have said or done something altogether indecent.'

Instinct took over from impotent thought and he crossed the space between them to where she sat and taking possession of her hands, he raised them to his lips. With honest depth of feeling he said, 'Helena, you *did* honour me and you must know it. I don't belong in your world and have nothing to offer you worth a minute's consideration. Such one-sided generosity is beyond me to accept. I'm a lawyer. In other words, a man in trade with a lot of hard work ahead of him. I live in two dreary rented rooms. Few, if any, women would care to share them and I told you the truth when some time ago I told you it would be ten years before I could think of marriage. Sorry though I am for it at this moment, I'm not the kind of man who could be content to be his wife's pensioner. As for your father – I can almost hear the tone in which he would order me off the premises if I were fool enough to apply to him for permission to marry his daughter and laid out for him what I can offer you.'

'What my father would say might surprise you.'

'I prefer not to put it to the test.'

Her smile was painful. 'That's the point, isn't it? You like me well enough, but not enough to marry me, even with the inducement of a large fortune. I ought to resent it – be furious – flay you with words. But what I want to do is burst into tears and howl like a spoiled three-year-old deprived of a treat she thought certain. In my case, not certain, just dimly hoped for.'

'If I have led you to think I hoped to marry you, I deserve to be hanged!'

She looked at him wryly, hunching her lilac-clad shoulders. 'No. You have been most careful to keep well away from giving any such impression. The fault is mine for thinking I could push you in the direction I wished you to go. Oh, well. . . .' She stood up from the swing with an air of decision. 'You would not think, would you, that I have been taught to lose gracefully? I am having little success in it on this occasion, though I'm doing the best I can.' She lifted a rueful face to his and on a lighter note said, 'Kiss me, my handsome young fellah. Please. Just this once to help me say goodbye to a dream.'

He hesitated but then did as she asked, not sure that he was not making a mistake. Her lips were soft, sweet and clinging, tempting him to deepen the kiss. He put the temptation firmly away and stood back from her.

She offered no resistance to his distancing himself, but there was a sudden swim of tears in her eyes and with soft, angry vehemence, she said, 'Damn you, Timothy Ryland. I take back my goodbye. If there's a way to *make* you love me, I'll find it! And if I can't make you love me, perhaps I can at least make you desire me. And that's more unmaidenly than anything else I've done or said!' She turned away and began to walk briskly back towards the house and as she did so the last gold of the day vanished.

For a moment or two he stood still then shook himself into action and followed. He caught up with her at the gate, pulled her arm through his and clamped it to his side before jerking the gate closed behind them.

She made no attempt to draw free and neither spoke until they reached the house. There, he held her to a stop again at the bottom of the steps to the door.

'Don't think I wasn't tempted, Helena. And not by the fortune. Are we still friends?'

Her eyes seemed to have retained some of the day's brilliance. They gleamed up at him and her smile was whitely feline. 'Oh, yes, I promise you that. But be warned, my fine young fellah, I shall be making plans. . . .'

CHAPTER TWELVE

A NOTE FROM Prue was delivered to Timothy's rooms two days after the Ambershaw gala day. It informed him that his father was making good progress and hoped to be allowed out of bed before long.

But, wrote Prue, *he still has you on his mind and is troubled by it. I know he wants to see you, so please come. The fret and worry of whatever it is can only hold back his full recovery. Whatever lies between you, Timothy, as a son you owe him a visit, but if more is wanted, come for my sake. Come on Sunday, neither of your brothers will be here; Andy is at sea and I have told Giles to keep away. . . .*

So on yet another Sunday, Timothy found himself riding to Blackthorns. The door of the cottage stood wide and as soon as he entered, Prue came into the passage. She smiled warmly at him. 'I knew you'd come.'

He smiled wryly at her. 'Whenever did your husband or your sons refuse you anything? You bewitch us all and you know it.'

'If that is true, you will make your peace with Josh. I expect you'll find him dozing, but go up to him anyway and settle his present worry if you can.'

He mounted the stairs and entered his parents' bedroom. The day was warm and Josh lay on his back under a sheet and blanket, the handsome patchwork quilt folded back over the end rails of the big bed. His eyes were closed. Timothy stood looking down at him, noting that his familiar, deep-dyed tan had paled a little and the shadows beneath his eyes were dark, giving him an unfamiliar look of weariness and strain. He looked older than he remembered. *A felled oak*, Timothy thought, and was caught unwittingly in the net of his old affection and admiration for his father. With almost womanly tenderness he put out a hand to wipe back the hair straying across Josh's brow. In that moment Josh's eyes flew open and like blue fire, the life behind them blazed up at him. Timothy snatched back his hand as though guilty of doing something discreditable and immediately was angry with himself and uncertain for what reason.

'*You*!' Josh said, surprise blending with the identification.

'You sent for me, so here I am.' Off-balance, Timothy spoke stiffly.

'I said I wished you'd come: there's a difference.'

'Either way, I'm here.' Why it was Timothy could not have said, but their words seemed to clash like swords in their initial, hostile engagement.

Josh moved restlessly in the bed. 'But not willingly. . . I remember you saying that. When was it? It's damnable how my memory comes and goes.'

'No, not willingly. With good reason. But as the runt of the family high-minded generosity is outside my compass.'

'Who said you were the runt of the family?'

'It is a long time since I was first made aware of it, though it was Andy who most recently reminded me. He thought he knew the answer to a particular question and wanted me to confirm it. He was wrong and I refused. He had difficulty restraining himself from pummelling me into giving him what he wanted.' Eyes glinting, he gave Josh a sardonic smile. 'It must be difficult to adapt to having a cuckoo in the nest. But then it isn't always easy for the cuckoo either. Especially when he turns out to be smaller than the rest of the brood. Your comfort must be that you have two sons made in your own image, both of whom think you without fault. I apologize for being odd man out, but I was born so.'

'You may not equal the size and strength of the other two, but you have your own weapons and know how to use them, don't you, Son?' Josh said bitterly.

'If runts are to survive they learn how early, or not at all.' He shrugged. 'However, I'm here today because my mother feels some thought of me is causing you distress. I am at a loss to know what it is this time.'

Josh frowned. '*The Joyous Lady* . . . when she ran aground, as I remember it, it was you brought me ashore. Others say different.'

'Andy brought you ashore. I arrived when things were all but over and purely by chance. What would I be doing aboard *The Joyous Lady*? I'm a lawyer, not a seaman. All I did was lead the horse that carried you from Rogan's Point to Blackthorns. Andy and Giles did everything else for you. Don't underrate it. Giles made it plain his teeth would be in my throat if I as much as laid a hand on you to help.'

'It's so clear in my mind,' Josh said fretfully.

'You dreamed it. From the time the mizzen came down you were never in your senses until long after you were in your bed. How could you know who did what for you?'

A lengthy silence and then, '*Timothy. . .* ?'

Timothy recognized the appeal in his father's voice, guessed what he was asking, but kept an unresponsive silence. Never again would he put himself in a vulnerable relationship with this man. The silence knotted with Josh's reluctance to put what else needed saying into words. Meeting neither help nor encouragement, he struggled through several long moments before he conceded, 'I made a mistake where you were concerned. A bad mistake.'

'Yes. But it clarified a number of things for me. Completed my education, you might say.' Quick, sharp-edged, unforgiving.

Josh scowled; said irritably, 'You never give an inch, do you, boy?' The blue gaze clung to his son's face, fierce with another question that needed to be asked. At last it burst from him in a hoarse whisper, 'Why haven't you told your brothers what happened between us?'

'For the same reason you haven't.'

'You can't know what my reason is.'

'Do you want me to put it into words?'

Staring up into the unyielding young face looking down at him, after a struggle, Josh said, 'No, damn you! You're too knowing by half. Impossible to talk to.' His scowl deepened. 'And why do you always think I want something from you? *Take what you want from me. . . .* You've said that more than once. What the devil do you think I want?'

'Ease for your conscience . . . a handy whipping-boy. . . the skin off my back. Anything . . . everything,' was the uncompromising answer he got.

What he wanted, Josh thought hopelessly, was what he himself had destroyed: the old trust and respect, and more than that, the old warmth of affection. He said, 'I think you'd better go.'

'Yes. There's no meeting place for us any more, is there? If, indeed, there ever was outside my imagination.' He turned and walked towards the door, stopped to look back and say, 'Remember though, anything you want that is due from me in duty as a son I will deliver.' In the doorway he turned again to add as quietly though in a quite different voice, 'But I shall not forget what is due between us as man and man. At the right time, that, too, I will deliver.'

It was no soothing promise to be left with. Word by word the rift between them had widened. Watching his son walk out of the room, Josh wondered from where the boy got the diamond-hard streak that made him so unreachable? The streak that he himself had uncovered, to his lasting regret. And he had more to regret than that. He had laid himself open to the boy's contempt by not telling his two older sons why he and Timothy were at odds. It had to be done and the sooner the better.

But with nothing to do but lie still and think over what had just passed, a sense of injury began to edge in. Enough was enough. He had made a mistake. What man gets through life without making a few? Resentment grew, took life. *Dammit, I've served my penance,* he told himself. *I'll put things straight with the older two, but then, young Timothy, you had better begin to walk a little more warily around me. . . .*

Prue waited for Timothy in the hallway, a look of hopeful expectancy on her face.

Timothy shook his head at her. 'I'm sorry, Mother. Between us, we've made things worse. We're too unlike. And mainly my fault this time, I admit. It was not my intention, but he brings out the worst in me.'

'It was not always so.'

'No. But I don't have the feeling for him I once had that would prevent it.'

'The trouble is not that you are too unlike, but that you are too *like* . . . slow to anger, but when you do, obstinate beyond reason, holding your opinions too dear, too extreme.'

'Then may God sort it for us.'

'He will. And perhaps not to your satisfaction.'

'I thought you said no aspect of your education had been neglected,' Perry said, as he and Timothy stood surveying the amenities of Ambershaws' handsome billiards room the following Sunday.

'Well, billiards appears to have been overlooked.'

'Then I had better do something to repair the omission.' He reached for a cue from a nearby rack and handed it to Timothy.

'That is a cue and you use it to strike such balls as I shall indicate into the pockets at the sides and corners of the table in the way I will show you. If in so doing you rip the baize, my father will have you roasted over a slow fire.'

'Thank you. How very encouraging.'

'It should aid your concentration.'

Some forty minutes later, with some grasp of the rules of billiards and a glimmering of what was needed to persuade the ball to travel in the desired direction, Timothy accepted with relief the wine Perry offered him.

Pouring a second glass, his back to his friend, Perry said with careful nonchalance, 'I spoke to my father about Miss Mariott a day or two before our gala day.'

'Oh?' It was not easy to keep the same evenness of tone; to sound no more than mildly interested.

'Yes. Because I'm the heir there are certain obligations. . . . Things expected. . . . Sometimes tiresome, but—' He shrugged an end to the sentence.

'And?' Timothy prompted.

'He said if I had fixed my heart on the girl and she was willing, he had no obstacle to place in the way of a match between us providing there was none on the Mariotts' side. He said he thought Miss Mariott would grace the position she would one day occupy if we made a match of it, but he said too, he hoped he and my mother might last out a few years yet before she had to take on that responsibility.'

Timothy did not need to look round to see the grin that accompanied the last words. Positioning balls for another game, he said, 'And Miss Mariott? What does she say?'

'Ah. That I don't know. I have yet to show her what I'm hoping for. Couldn't be too open about it until I'd spoken to my father. And she's so young. I feel I have to go gently with her . . . be careful not to rush her.' He paused, said with unusual earnestness, 'She means a great deal to me, Timothy. Wish me luck.'

Luck! He was born to it! How much more did he think he needed? Ashamed of the sourness of his thought, Timothy turned and trying to infuse some warmth into his voice, said, 'Of course. All the luck you need . . . or think you do.'

'I shall have to tackle Rebecca's father next. I've met him briefly once or twice, but haven't really got his measure. Deep and dark, I've thought. In other words, reserved and a little severe. You've known him a long time. What do you think?'

'Deep and dark . . . and the best of good friends.'

'Yes, of course. I was forgetting. He and your father go back a long, long way.'

'Through thick and thin. Nick shot my father once to keep him from falling into a naval trap during the coastal blockade. Andy had been used as bait and Nick had a good idea how Josh would tackle the problem – head on, as always. He's quickly beyond reason if any of us, the family I mean, is under threat. Josh wasn't grateful. Having the responsibility taken from him cut deep into his pride and he swore he'd kill Nick for taking over. Some while later, he got Nick to the point where he thought it about to happen. But what Father wanted was to give Nick what he saw as a well-deserved fright.'

His mind locked on his own problem, Perry let that pass without comment. 'You've known her a long time . . . do you think she'll have me?' he asked.

It would be harder, Timothy thought, to think of any reason why she would not. With a struggle to keep bitterness out of his voice, he said, 'I can think of no reason why she should not.'

'Because of my future rank?' Perry had his own reasons for bitterness.

'It can't lessen your attraction, but I hope you think better of Becca than to believe it would sway her.'

'No. I don't think she gives it a thought. It was a stupid question.'

Timothy left Ambershaws in an unsettled frame of mind.

Perry was pushing things along at what seemed to him all too fast a rate. He knew it wasn't so. It was just that he himself wanted nothing definite to happen. While things remained static, he could still fool himself that one day, by some miracle, Becca would be his.

CHAPTER THIRTEEN

IT WAS THOUGHT appropriate by the Mariotts to invite the senior as well as the junior members of the Osmond family to the next ball they planned to give. The invitations were gracefully accepted by all. A flurry of activity resulted: Elise and her cook devised the most tempting diversity of refreshments they could think of. The house, always shiningly clean, was polished again from attics to cellars and on the morning of the event the garden was denuded of all its choicest blooms to the despair of the gardener and his assistant.

But the Osmonds were destined not to come. The sudden death of the earl's younger brother in a riding accident the day before the event, put the Osmond family into mourning and attending the Mariotts' ball out of the question.

Timothy came, though not without some misgiving. He had met Rebecca two or three times since she had struck him, but it had always been in the company of other people. Usually they were Perry and Helena and it was they who decided the pairing.

For the first hour or two of the evening after his stiff exchange of greetings with Becca, Timothy was careful not to allow himself to be close enough either to dance with her, or to be under the necessity of falling into conversation with her. For all that, he could not keep himself from watching her, with love and with need. But inseparable from those, were anger and bitterness. The bitterness was that of loss: she would marry Perry and put herself forever out of his reach. The anger was something quite different: though he would have stood between her and any threat on earth, he felt an intense and ever-growing desire to call her to account for the unprovoked blow she had given him. During the two months that lay between that occasion and now, the memory had festered in him like a neglected wound. It was not something he could leave forever in limbo, passed over, ignored. Everything between them had come to a halt with that blow. Understanding was necessary to him and with half the evening gone he decided there was no point in leaving it any longer.

He crossed the room to where Rebecca stood bending to speak to an elderly woman comfortably seated on one of the small, gilt sofas set against the wall. Her gown, new for the occasion, was of pale coral-coloured barége, the three tiers of its skirt edged with prettily embroidered violet satin ribbon, the low neckline flounced and edged in the same way. Her back was turned to the room.

'Miss Mariott.'

She straightened and, holding herself very stiffly erect, turned to face him.

He had chosen his moment with care. The orchestra was playing the introductory bars to a waltz. 'May I have the pleasure—' The conventional invitation in a flat tone from which nothing could be read. With no absolute confidence that she would take it, he held out a hand to her.

Apprehension flickered briefly in her eyes, but she laid her hand in his as though compelled; as though she, too, felt that tonight discussion of what lay between them could not be evaded. She kept her gaze lowered as he swung her into the dance. Neither spoke, but three times in the first few minutes she missed her step and stumbled.

He knew what he wanted to say, but knew too, that it could not be said here in the midst of other people's conversation, the insistent music and the need to follow it. The invitation had been to detach her from whomever she happened to be with. Purposefully, he danced her to that part of the room where a door opened into the hall, took one of her hands firmly in his and said, 'Come. We have to talk.'

From the hall he guided her into the book-room, where, because it was also Nick's study, there would be a fire at this time of the year. Because there was no expectation that the room would be used that evening, neither lamps nor candles had been lit, and though what was left of the day's fire was declining towards extinction, the small remaining glow was sufficient to guide them through its well-known features. Timothy fed a few smaller pieces of wood from the nearby basket into the heart of the fire's redness and because some were resinous there was an almost instant flare of light. It was enough to allow them to see each other as clearly as they needed.

Becca, Timothy saw, was forcing herself to meet his gaze, doing her best to appear at ease and leaving it to him to break the silence. The effect was that she looked very much as she had looked as a child when conscious of being at fault and expecting a scold. Memory moved him to tenderness. He clamped down on it. This was no time to show weakness.

He said sternly, 'I can see you know what I am going to ask you, Becca – why did you do it?'

She knew at once what he meant and gazed at him with helpless uncertainty. She had no prepared answer, true or false. He saw it and wondered that she found it so difficult.

Rebecca thought despairingly, how can I say, *because I love you . . . because I hate you . . . because you don't love me?* But in using her first name he had given her opportunity for a diversion and she seized it to say coldly, 'I think you forget yourself, Mr Ryland. I am *Miss Mariott* to you.'

He dipped his head ironically. 'Miss Mariott, then . . . I should be grateful if would give me a reason for the blow you struck me.'

Inspiration refused any assistance. She clung to the haughtiness of her earlier response to him and said with assumed indifference, 'I suppose I had a reason. But it was some time ago. I have no memory of it.' She shrugged dismissively.

He took a step towards her. 'Stop playing games, Becca – Miss Mariott, I mean. It was a punitive blow, intended to be remembered. You had come into the room too recently for me to have offended you that day. Therefore the reason for the blow must have arisen on some other occasion. I cannot think what or when, but I need to understand.' His mouth twisted. 'I prefer not to offend again and attract a like punishment.'

Unable to sustain the role she had chosen, she dropped it and let her frustration colour her answer. 'If I told you, you still would not understand.'

'Why should I not?'

'Because you're a man.'

He drew a quick, impatient breath. 'Impossible to argue with. But I've known you a long time, Becca, so try me. I might surprise you.'

She had gone as near as she dared to telling him what he wanted to know and now, rabbit-like, she dodged back into cover. 'I wish you will not use my first name. You chose to discard its use. I accepted the change and now I prefer it so. You are Mr Ryland to me.'

'I find calling you Becca a difficult habit to break. I think I made a mistake.'

'The fact that we are no longer friends should remind you.'

'Very well. But our parents are friends and our meeting from time to time cannot be avoided. The Osmonds also regard us as making the natural parts of a foursome. We have to maintain at least the appearance of friendly acquaintance.'

'I shall do my best in that direction.' She remembered then how much she owed him and, genuinely grateful, she said more naturally, 'I made use of you once and I am truly sorry for having done so. You were more than kind to support me as you did and I am more grateful than you can know.' It seemed less than adequate for what he had done and she sought for something to add. All she could think of was to give him the only thing she thought he wanted which was to know that she was severing the claims she had laid on him. Beginning in a small voice, she said, 'When I returned from Italy, you made me see the need for me to learn to be more independent . . . not to lean on you as I did when a child. I realized too, it was unwise of me to expect the affection you had for me then to last into adulthood.' She pushed hair back from her face in a gesture he remembered as belonging very much to her childhood. She drew herself up and lifted her chin and those movements too, were familiar. 'My own feelings are changing, too. I am beginning to learn the difference between the blind hero-worship of childhood and the more measured judgements one makes as experience enlarges one's view. The best answer I can give to the question of why I struck you is that it was probably a last display of immaturity. At least, I hope it was the last.'

He recognized that she was trying to carry things off in good style but chiefly succeeding in reminding him how young she was. For a moment or two he was very much in sympathy with Prescott who had been driven to shake her. He had tried to convince her that he wanted to be free of her childhood's adoration of him, and now, having succeeded, he knew how very little he truly wanted it.

With a small tremble in her voice, she finished, 'I expect as time goes on our ways will diverge more and more. I shall grow more sensible. Perhaps even begin to wonder what it was I saw in you that I thought you such a paladin. It will be better so, won't it?' She glanced round a little helplessly then, as though anxious for this wretched meeting to come to an end, but uncertain how to accomplish it. Taking a deep breath, she looked back at him and said with a pale smile, 'Now if you please, I should like to return to the ballroom.'

If she had given him the explanation he wanted it had already slipped away from him. What was clear in his mind was the cheerless prospect of their future relationship: a relationship dwindling into a vague smiling wonder that it had once meant so much. On her side it was all too likely. On his, he could not see beyond the pain of loss. Now it was he who wanted to cling to the past; wanted to take her in his aims and kiss her, not only into something close to the old warmth of feeling, but into what would take them on into something stronger, deeper and altogether more passionate – and lasting.

He turned to the door, opened it and waited for her to pass through. He took her back to her mother's side, and made an excuse not to linger. Having put the width of the room between them, he found a quiet corner where he could stand and savour to the full what he had achieved. A distance between them – yes – because it was necessary for her sake. But to decline into a mere childish memory? No. Irrational, it might be, but he wanted more from her than that.

He was not left long in contemplation of his own affairs. Mr and Mrs Lasseter were among the guests and Ralph Lasseter was not one to allow an opportunity to discuss *his* affairs pass unused, whatever the occasion. Seeing Timothy alone, he came across to speak to him about the recent discovery of gold in California and what effect it might have on certain of his investments.

It was some time before Lasseter set Timothy free and then it was in one of the brief intervals between the dances. Like someone caught in an enchantment, Timothy's gaze immediately went in search of Becca's coral gown. He found it at the southern end of the room. Her back was to the fireplace there and she appeared to be listening to an eagerly gesticulating young man who was describing some scene or happening that had roused him to enthusiasm. He looked, Timothy thought as the gesticulations got wilder, as though he had sampled the Mariotts' wine with much the same enthusiasm. With acute irritation he saw Becca step back to avoid a flying hand. The oaf was making a nuisance of himself, and he was debating whether or not to break in on the pair when there was a small flare of light behind Becca that flickered uncertainly, but did not quite disappear. The swing of her skirts as she moved to avoid the young man's hand had taken it too near the burning coals, he suspected. The fire had reached for it, had a small hold and without doubt, was seeking a greater.

At that moment the band struck up for the next dance and people began to drift on to the dancing floor. Thrusting ruthlessly through the thickening crowd without pausing to make apologies, he rushed to reach her before the gown engulfed her in flame.

She seemed still unaware when he reached her and his expression alarmed her, so that she shrank from him. Reaching out he seized her firmly by the shoulder and roared at her to stand still. Spinning her round, he wrenched and tore at her skirt to detach it from the tight bodice, desperately screwing the flaring silk of the layered material between his hands to prevent it igniting her underskirts. He could not save the delicate, lace-trimmed lawn petticoat that she wore between gown and crinoline, but he did prevent the crinoline itself from taking fire. The heavier flax and horsehair garment that supported the spread of her gown could have charred and sunk against her flesh doing dreadful damage.

In the first bewildered moments, Becca had fought him, but as she realized what was happening she gasped with horror and submitted totally to his efforts. When the danger was past, the coral gown and first petticoat were utterly ruined, but the number of petticoats women wore those days, together with the speed with which Timothy had acted, had saved Rebecca from injury.

Nick and Elise reached their daughter's side as the last smouldering remnants were ripped from her. Nannibet, always watching her pet charge from some secluded vantage point, arrived a minute later with a cloak of Nick's to cover Becca's dishevelment and allow her to walk from the room with no embarrassing display of undergarments. More and more guests had crowded round to see what could be seen and Timothy was able to edge out from among them and walk out of the room without attracting notice.

From there, he escaped into the Mariotts' latest improvement to the house, a large cloakroom incorporating one of the very newest Bramah flush WCs and a porcelain basin with running water. By the time he reached it pain was concentrating his attention on his hands and he had taken in the scorched state of the cuffs of both his shirt and evening jacket.

Seeking relief for his hands, he filled the basin with cold water and gingerly slid his burnt and blistered fingers into it.

Nick came looking for him and insisted on seeing the damage. 'I suppose you're intending to ride back to your rooms with the reins between your teeth.'

'Oh, a good soak should cool them down and maybe depress the blisters.'

'It may help. It's not a cure. I've already sent someone for a measure of brandy and some straws through which to drink it. That, too, will be a help, not a cure. When the man comes, I'll tell him to send one of the grooms for Dr Bartlett to dress your hands properly. After that you can take your pick of the spare bedrooms and tomorrow we'll see how things are.'

'Tomorrow I have work to do.'

'There may be work to be done, but it's unlikely you'll be

doing it, or only with the help of an amanuensis. Tonight, as I said, you'll be staying here if I have to lock you in a room and set my strongest man to guard the door.'

Timothy's laugh was tinged with bitterness. 'You're confusing me with my brothers. It would not take your *strongest* man to contain me, but I won't put you to so much trouble. I'm grateful.'

Nick gave him a sardonic look. '*You're* grateful! Tell me how many more ways is Rebecca to put herself in your debt? And Elise and I along with her? The girl could have died hideously in tonight's little crisis, or been disfigured for life. Am I allowed to thank you for saving her from either disaster?'

'I hope you won't think it necessary. What else would I, or anyone else, do who saw her gown catch fire? I happened to be watching the antics of the clown talking to her when it happened. Anyone would have done what I did.'

'*That*, we may thank Heaven we did not have to prove. My wonder is that after the blow she gave you, you did not let her burn.'

'Oh, I talked to Becca about that earlier. It's all in the past.'

'Is it! Then I hope you'll share with me the reason behind it, because she has never been able to explain it to either her mother or to me. I have examined every possibility I have been able to imagine without finding one that fitted the case.'

'I cannot help you. She could not tell me *because*, she said, *I would not understand*. Because I am a man.' Timothy's tone was wry.

Nick made an impatient sound in his throat. 'It is probably *she* who cannot understand. Is that all she said?'

'It is all I remember.'

'Then all *I* can say is, thank God my other two children are boys. I don't think I could long survive another girl.'

Nick turned away as a servant came in with the brandy, gave the man a message for one of the grooms, turned back to

Timothy and said, 'Now drink this. I'll put it here within reach. Nobody will be watching you, so you may be as vulgar as you please in drinking it. I must get back to the other guests, but you may rely on Elise wanting to see you.'

'Tell her I don't want to be thanked, I beg you.'

Nick nodded. 'I'll tell her, but how much notice she'll take I can't promise.' He walked to the door, looked back and said, 'You're a damned difficult fellow, Timothy Ryland, but you'll do at a pinch.'

CHAPTER FOURTEEN

TIMOTHY WAS UP before it was light the next morning. In spite of the doctor's careful anointing of his hands, the thick padding and final bandaging, the pain had quietened only enough to allow him to sleep in fitful snatches. He had removed his jacket, but could manage no more and had lain on top of the bedclothes with the quilt to cover him. He shrugged his way back into his jacket and with the less badly damaged first finger and thumb of his left hand, even managed to get two buttons into their holes. That was all he could do towards his morning grooming. Unwashed and unshaven he went down the stairs, found a maidservant and left his thanks and excuses for Elise and Nick, tacking to them his hope that Miss Mariott was none the worse for what had happened.

He let himself out of the house into the grey dimness that gave some promise of dawn and went to the stables with no certainty of his ability to ride the five miles to the livery stables, but hopeful of the docile hack's willing co-operation. If he had to, he would walk and lead the horse.

Early as it was, Nick's head groom, John Hammond, was in the stableyard to greet him, looking much as he always had except that his once thick thatch now only fringed his balding head, its colour nearer to white than grey.

'Master said you might be wanting to go back to Chichester

early. The pony's all ready to put to the gig and I'm to drive you there myself The livery horse'll go quiet enough behind, I shouldn't wonder.'

Nick knew him better than he had realized and Timothy was thankful for it. The roan pony, fresh and ready for exercise, covered the five miles smartly and Hammond left Timothy at the livery stables to return his hired mount and settle his bill. He walked the short distance to his rooms afterwards and there, with some difficulty, changed into clothes suitable for the office. He then sought out a barber's shop where he could get shaved, washed, buttoned and brushed into neatness before seeking out his usual breakfast café. His food was cut up for him by the motherly and inquisitive waitress, which made him all the more thankful to be able to empty the coffee-pot she set on the table without help if not without discomfort.

Arriving at the office, he found Nick was again ahead of him, having sent a note to Mr Diment's home to explain Timothy's damaged hands, not trusting Timothy to give an adequate explanation. The result was that a sensible, clerk-apprentice, named Harvey, had been assigned to him to undertake all work involving the use of his hands. The only disadvantage was to find himself regarded as something of a hero.

About noon, a very light tap on the door was followed by it opening before he could give permission. He came swiftly to his feet and his voice on the edge of dismay, said, 'Becca!' and as swiftly corrected himself, 'Miss Mariott, I should say.'

Given a nod of dismissal, the clerk set a chair for the visitor and regretfully, took himself out of the room.

'You're not here alone, I trust,' Timothy said severely, annoyed with himself for not having anticipated this particular visitor.

'No. I left Nannibet downstairs, well within call should I need her. So I think I am safe from any unbridled expression of your feelings,' she told him tartly.

He let that pass and asked formally, 'How can I help you?'

She sighed. 'Oh, Timothy! Do you really expect me to ignore what you did for me last night?' Her gaze fell to the bandages. 'They tell me you crushed out the flames between your hands and tore at the burning silk without any regard for what you were doing to yourself.'

'People make the most of any story. Don't make still more of it.'

'Well, the flames did not put themselves out and from what remained of my dress and petticoat they had been well alight. And you worked so fast I had not the smallest scorching on my skin. I shudder when I think what it would have been like if you had not come to my rescue.'

'Someone would have done what I did. It was just chance that I was the first to notice what was happening.'

'So you say. I am just thankful I did not have to wait for that someone to come. Am I not allowed to say thank you?'

'Bec—' He shook his head in irritation at his inability to remember the change he had brought about. 'Miss Mariott, what you have said is thanks enough. So please say no more.'

That struck a spark. 'You do like to lay down the law, don't you?' And then realizing what she had said, she laughed. 'Well, I suppose you would, being a lawyer. But it is a little irksome to the rest of us at times.'

'Well, lawyers are a tedious lot at best.'

She sighed and fell to smoothing her gloves over her fingers. Silence held them both. After a time, she said, 'It wasn't easy for me last night.'

'What wasn't?'

'Saying what I did. But it seemed to be what you wanted to hear. I thought that if I could not please you any other way I could do *that*. And I do understand why you want to change things between us since Edward Jordan and the baby and everything. But I still find it hard.'

He wanted to say, *I don't give a toss for Edward Jordan or the baby. I'd beg you to marry me if I had anything to offer and if Perry Osmond were not there to offer you far more than most men can.*

He sat back in his chair and looked at her, unable to think of anything else to say. She was a distracting presence even in the plain mulberry-coloured, high-necked woollen gown she was wearing. The quilted velvet, three-quarter coat she had on over it was of a near indigo hue which her bonnet matched, though that was enlivened by a blue ribbon and a cluster of bright feathers. But the generally sober colours did nothing to lessen her beauty, or hide the fact that the bonnet framed what was to him, the most beautiful face in the world – certainly, the best-loved. She had been woven into his life since he was ten years old and now was so threaded through his mind, his dreams, his desires, that she was a necessary part of the whole, impossible to separate from Timothy Ryland without causing lasting damage. But this was his workplace and the sooner she left it the better for the peace of his soul! Except that, as always, the last thing he wanted was for her to go.

He dragged his gaze away to look down at his desk. Flatly, he said, 'Do not concern yourself about the unhappy past. It weighs nothing with me. But you should not be here, you know. It is a place of business.'

She thought him contemptuous and it seemed to her that she could never draw the response she wanted from him. Indignantly, she blurted, '*Oh, Timothy*! Must you despise me so much! Do you think I wanted to be raped? To find myself carrying a stranger's baby? To be faced with my father's anger? My mother's distress? And to crown it, your contempt?' She felt tears constricting her throat, pricking under her eyelids, and fought to hold them contained, determined not to cry.

'Becca, Becca. . . I am not – have never been contemptuous of you. Far from it' He felt again the murderous surge of rage he felt whenever he remembered Edward Jordan. But for her sake and his own, he could not allow the threat and swell of emotion between them any further increase. Above all, he could not do as he wanted and take her in his arms and prove to her how very different his feelings for her were from those he had made her believe were his. With a coolness he was far from feeling, he said, 'I think I should call Nannibet to you.' Giving her no chance to protest, he rose as he spoke and going to the door called down to Harvey to ask Miss Mariott's companion to come up and to send someone to the livery stable to tell them the Mariott carriage was wanted.

Turning back from the door, he saw that somehow she had imposed control on herself, though her eyes were overbright and the smile she conjured up was unstable.

'Yes, I must go. I am intruding on your working day. I just felt I could not allow time to pass before expressing my gratitude for what you did for me.' It sounded wretchedly cold and formal, but he had made it plain enough that the last thing he wanted was an outpouring of the fullness of her gratitude.

She heard Nannibet lumber up the last few stairs and rising to her feet, gave him a small curtsy that touched the edge of mockery. 'Goodbye, Mr Ryland. I hope your hands recover soon. Remember me with kindness when you can.' She turned to the door and waved to Nannibet to go down again. 'We're off. The carriage will be at the door by now. Mr Ryland is nothing if not efficient in all he does.'

Chichester managed to look as cold and bleak as the easterly wind that blew in erratic gusts, seeming to come from nowhere and go nowhere, but chilling to the bone the few people who walked its streets in the afternoon of the first Wednesday in November. Timothy and Perry, coming from the warmth of The Ship's restaurant were glad to step into the partial shelter of the high walls that enclosed Knockangle Lane. A narrow alley, it allowed room for two to walk abreast comfortably but no more. Perry had extracted Timothy from his office on legitimate business, but the consultation had taken place over lunch in the comfortable ambience of The Ship.

The dullness of the day and the high walls made early twilight here and it took a moment or two for Timothy to recognize the tall figure advancing towards them in seaman's rig of reefer jacket, duck trousers and proofed boots as his father.

He had only a few seconds then to decide how to meet the problem so suddenly presented. Hastily, he reviewed his choices. If he passed Josh with no more recognition than he had given him outside the corn chandler's a year ago and Perry subsequently discovered his identity, it would be reasonable for Perry to assume that he, Timothy, was ashamed of his origins. He was not and pride forbade that anyone should think so. If he behaved as he would in normal circumstances and stopped to greet his father and introduce him to Perry, he placed himself entirely in Josh's hands. He decided he preferred to take his chance on that to giving anyone, including Josh – no, especially Josh! – the impression he thought himself superior to his family.

As the distance between them closed, he slowed to a halt and said with some slight awkwardness, 'Father! An unexpected meeting. I'm glad to see you up and about.' Surprising him, he realized that much was true.

Josh's gaze, meeting his, was both wary and quizzical, but all he said was 'Timothy. . . .'

Timothy turned to his companion. 'Perry, may I have the pleasure of introducing my father to you?'

There was a tension in the air that did not escape Perry, though he learned nothing from Timothy's expression. 'The pleasure will be mine,' he said with his engaging smile.

'Perry – my father, Joshua Ryland. Father – Lord Osmond.' He left it at that.

Josh took the introduction in his stride, inclining his head and saying simply, 'My lord.'

Perry held out his hand. 'Timothy failed to claim me as his friend, sir, but I claim him as mine and hope that gives me the right to invite you to call me Perry as he does.'

'Thank you. Timothy is fortunate in his friends, whatever misfortune he meets with in other directions.' Taking Perry's hand, Josh slid a far from guileless glance in his son's direction.'

That there was an uneasy tension threaded through the meeting, Perry was aware and sensing that they were about to be engulfed in an awkward silence, he said smoothly, 'Although you and I have not met before, Mr Ryland, I believe you and my father are acquainted. The particular brandy he prefers is much appreciated by his friends.'

Josh smiled in his comfortable way. 'His lordship and I have met upon occasion, but I am better acquainted with his butler.' Josh's glance took in his son's careful lack of expression and added, 'Now, if you will excuse me, I am already late for an appointment.' He shared a nod between them. 'Perry . . . Timothy,' and walked on.

If Perry hoped Timothy might explain the mystery of what lay between himself and his father, he was disappointed. He would not allow himself to ask any intrusive questions, but he remained curious.

The honours of the meeting had gone to Josh, Timothy thought. He had responded with grace, followed his son's lead, and it was only Timothy who could read the possibility of his remark about 'friends' being in any way equivocal. Josh had not sought to make capital out of the exchange. He had played fair.

As he always did, damn him! Timothy thought, *if one excepted one memorable occasion when he had used his superior strength to flog his son without even questioning his guilt. Admirable he was in may ways but he was still the man who had readily accepted that he, Timothy, was capable of a despicable betrayal of a generous friend and his guileless and trusting young daughter.*

CHAPTER FIFTEEN

IT WAS MID-NOVEMBER before Perry, Becca, Helena and Timothy were able to arrange another meeting at Ambershaws. By that time the earl's brother had been interred in the family vault and Timothy's hands had healed leaving him with one or two fading scars and some increased sensitivity between certain of his fingers. All of which, he had been assured, would vanish in time.

Following his uncle's funeral, Perry had been kept busy either standing in for his father while the earl was absent attending to various matters consequent upon the suddenness of his brother's death, or else was despatched to deputize for his father if the earl found it inconvenient to attend to the business himself.

Their meeting, however, was not allowed to stand unchanged: one more urgent call for help from the new widow necessitated Perry being sent to answer it and Timothy arrived to find himself the only guest. A last minute message sent to Danesfield had warned Rebecca of Perry's absence and decided her against going.

Because the days were short, it was a late morning meeting and he and Helena lunched in a small room off the conservatory. The servants passing in and out of the room robbed their tête-à-tête meal of any sense of intimacy and there was nothing to put the least ripple on the surface of their comfort.

'We are going to walk through the woods this afternoon,' Helena announced, when they sat finishing the last of the Tokay that been served with the fruit which ended the meal. 'I want to show you our gazebo. That's what we call it, though the views were lost long ago and it is far too old and rugged to have been built as a gazebo. It has the appearance of having started life as a keep, though Ambershaws has never been fortified. But little seems to be known of its history.'

It was a windy day and the shelter of the trees was welcome to both, though Helena wore a fur-lined cloak and Timothy a warm ulster. The keep transmuted to a gazebo stood, grey and stark, on a mound in a clearing. Steps to the entrance had been cut into the turf and what repairs had been made to the structure had been made with care to ensure there was small change to its original appearance. The door opened easily to Helena's touch. *Well oiled*, Timothy thought and smiled to himself. Everything belonging to the Earl of Ambershaw was well oiled, well maintained: it was what money and good management did for him.

There was one room at ground level. Opposite the door, rugged stone steps rose to the floor above; a thick, soft rope fastened to the wall gave aid to climbing and could be grasped for reassurance if needed. Air and a meagre allowance of natural light came in through the loopholes that might be supposed to have given passage in the past to the arrows of defenders of its thick stone walls. Provision had been made for their present visit; a glowing charcoal brazier, stood on a low stone dais in one corner spreading enough warmth to counteract what Timothy suspected would otherwise have been a tomb-like chill.

Helena waved a dismissive hand towards the steps. 'There's nothing more above than what amounts to a platform from which to take in the view, which is attractive but by no means impressive. There must have been much longer views at one time when the place was used for the purpose for which it was built and before the trees were allowed to grow up around it. The light is already too poor to see anything worth looking at, though.'

She walked into the centre of the room as she spoke and Timothy followed her.

'Would you light the lamp?' she said across her shoulder. 'There are tapers in the yellow pot on the table which you can light from the brazier.' She turned back as he went towards the table and as soon as he had a taper flaring she closed the door on the world outside.

'There! See how different it looks now,' she said pleasurably, as the lamp bloomed into golden light. 'Nothing like what the grim exterior leads one to expect.' Proprietary pleasure warmed her tone.

It was true. There were gay hangings on the walls, a chaise longue supported a bright crop of cushions, two or three comfortable-looking chairs waited for occupants around a solid rustic table and some hanging shelves accommodated a spirit-lamp, a tea and coffee-pot and flower-decorated cups and saucers. The warm glow of the lamp accentuated the comfort.

'If I had thought of it, I would have told them to leave water here which would have enabled me to offer you tea or coffee. Alas, I didn't.'

Helena was moving restlessly round the room as she spoke, touching various things as though renewing acquaintance with them and speaking in nervous bursts. It was plain to Timothy that something was disturbing her usual calm. Watching her with smiling amusement, he rested his lean elegant length against the rustic table and waited for her to reveal what it was.

As though suddenly conscious of her uneasy activity, Helena plumped down on the chaise longue and fell silent. Close to laughter, Timothy offered no help but let the silence run on until it reached the point of awkwardness and Helena said in a curiously defiant tone, 'If I told you we are now locked in here and no one will come to let us out until my reputation is thoroughly compromised, you would have no option as a gentleman but to marry me, would you? What have you say to that?'

Timothy laughed. 'First, that I am not a gentleman and second, that I am not easily coerced.'

Helena regarded him challengingly. 'My father could bring pressure to bear on you. And on your partners. You would need to take those things into consideration.'

Timothy kept his smile, but a glitter came into his green eyes. He stared silently at her for a long moment or two, then said quietly, but with no hint of amusement left in his voice, 'Well, let us suppose for a moment that he succeeded in forcing me into marriage with you. What *you* would need to take into consideration is what your life would be like afterwards . . . the hell I could make of it for you.'

Clearly she had not thought of that and gazed at him long and speculatively before saying, 'You could, of course, but would you?'

'Yes. Don't doubt it.' His voice was still quiet, but too positive to be questioned.

Forlornly, Helena said, 'Oh, Timothy, why can't you love me a little? I'm sure we could live a pleasant life together. I would try hard to be a good lawyer's wife.'

'I do love you, Helena, but as a very good friend. It would not be enough to make marriage between us work, my dear. You would be unspeakably bored within a year.'

'If we could only *try*.'

'And what then? A divorce? I can't see your father countenancing that.' He moved to sit down on the chaise longue beside her and took one of her hands in his. 'Helena, I am both touched and flattered that you should you want to marry me, but it would be disastrous, as you would soon discover. One day you will make a brilliant marriage with a man of your own order and you'll be glad I did not take advantage of your romantic generosity.'

She snatched her hand away. 'Now you're treating me like a child.'

'No. I'm pointing out that I would never be able to give you the kind of life that would make you happy. The kind of life to which you belong and which you have been bred to grace. The novelty might amuse you for a time, but then you would begin to find the limitations unbearable. You don't really know me; you only think that you do. As I said, you are a dear friend and perhaps something more than that. But you would not find it enough to make an enduring marriage and you would soon be hating me. The right man will seek you out one day, perhaps to make you a duchess.' He laughed. 'When that happens, think of all the good you could do me.'

'You're determined to break my heart.'

'I'm determined to stop you breaking it on a dream – a false dream.'

She looked at him, her eyes shining with tears. 'It should be easy to hate you! And how I wish it were!'

'I would rather you did not go so far as that.'

She shook her head frustratedly. 'It ought to be easy, but it isn't. But again, how I wish it were!'

'Please don't. You are a very special person, with a very special place in my affections, but I would be cheating you if I pretended a passion I don't feel . . . a love that is not the kind you want and deserve.'

She looked at him with helpless bafflement. 'Oh, you're so reasonable, you're inhuman! Everything you say is so sensible. Have you no passion? Do you never lose control? Never feel rage? Have you never loved or hated someone? Or never so strongly it seems as though it must burst through your breast if you don't find an outlet for it At the risk of shocking you, I tell you, Timothy, I would give you my body here and now if I thought it would make any difference to you. I swear to you what I feel for you is no timid, romanticized idea. I love you. Truly.'

He moved now to lay two fingers across her mouth. 'Don't, my dear. Please don't say any more, or you *will* come to hate me. If that happened, I would be ashamed and hate myself for giving you cause.'

She brushed his hand aside. 'You raised no objections when I suggested Perry was in love with Rebecca Mariott. Said nothing about *their* difficulties. Why is it so different for us?'

'Setting aside any difference in what they feel for each other, the difference in standing between Perry and Becca is not so great. She could step up into his life without meeting any enormous change from that to which she is accustomed. *You* would be stepping down and across a far greater divide if you married me. You would find yourself in a different world, one about which you know nothing, but which you would find unendurable after a while. King Cophetua and the beggar-maid in reverse is unworkable.'

She could think of nothing more to offer and he walked to the door and turned the ring-latch. The door did not move. He looked round at her.

His voice suddenly flat and hard, he said, 'So it wasn't a hypothetical situation you put forward.'

Helena made no reply.

His expression altered. In a voice that cut like a whip, he said, 'If you have the key you would be wise to give it to me at once.'

Trying to brave it out, she shrugged her shoulders.

He closed half the distance between them, menace in every purposeful line of his body before he came to a sudden stop as though forcing restraint on himself. 'Are you inviting me to look for it?' he demanded.

'*You wouldn't*!' Startled and dismayed, she stared at him.

The first unrelenting stride he took towards her forced her capitulation. Throwing up a hand as though to ward him off, she cried, 'No. No. I don't have it.'

'You are too intelligent not to have made provision to escape this situation, so where is it?'

The Timothy she was seeing now was not one she had ever glimpsed before. Her resistance collapsed suddenly and completely. 'My footman has it. I dropped it out of one of the loopholes. If a white handkerchief is waved out of the loophole over there' – she pointed – 'the door will be unlocked.' She spoke between resignation and sulk.

He did not immediately go where she indicated but came to where she sat and pulled her to her feet. His hands on her shoulders, he said, 'I am supposing that is the truth. Don't risk playing a second trick on me. A man in a temper is not always a rational being and men of my sort do not take kindly to being bested.'

Looking up into his less threatening face, she said, 'I can't believe you would hurt me.'

'My dear, you walked closer to the edge of danger than you know. Even at cost to myself I will not be coerced. I have two older brothers. Very early I realized I was differently built and would never reach their size and power; could never win against either in a trial of strength. I learned other ways of winning and how to endure if I could not.' He took a handkerchief out of his pocket. 'Now, if I wave this, who will come?'

'Dickon. He's my personal footman.'

'The man's a fool. You should have one with more sense.'

'His first loyalty is to me. He does what I tell him.'

'Two fools together then.' He saw her chin tilt haughtily. 'Dear Helena, you took a risk you don't understand. Don't ever do anything like this again to any man. Promise me.'

Pride was waking to stiffen her. 'I haven't wanted – or found the need – to trap a man into proposing to me before. But if it will cut the lecture, then I promise.'

'That's better. That sounds more like Lady Helena Osmond.'

'I think I'm beginning to hate you after all.'

He grinned at her. 'Good. Kept under control, a little hating won't do any harm.' He walked to the loophole she had indicated and extending his arm through the aperture, waved the handkerchief. That done, he returned to where Helena had reseated herself.

'Come. Head up. Let Dickon see his mistress in at least apparent triumphant control of the situation.'

'He won't be visible.'

'Just as well. I might exceed my prerogative and instruct him in his duties which I'm certain include a certain amount of protection.'

After a few minutes, he tried the door again and it opened at once. Under the trees on the path back to Ambershaws, it was dark enough to make it necessary to take her arm in his. She walked beside him in silence for some distance, then without looking at him, said, 'You would not really have searched my person if I had admitted to having the key on me and refused to give it to you, would you, Timothy?'

He was slow to reply, but said finally, 'That is not a question I am prepared to answer, but you would be wise to think that I might have done so.'

'I cannot imagine you doing anything so, so—'

'So ungentlemanly? I told you, you don't know me. I am not a gentleman. I was not bred to be one, though my parents kept firm hands on their male brood.'

'Perry would have killed you, if you had.'

'Perry might have tried. Do you want to set us all at each other's throats?'

'There you are again – so reasonable.'

'Very boring. It's what I'm trained to be. Think what you've escaped. And now that I have time to consider, I do not believe you would have called on your father's power to gain what you wanted. It would not be worthy of the Lady Helena I know.'

'Oh well. . . . I had to appear to have some worthwhile ammunition.' Her attempt at a smile went a little awry. 'But all to no purpose as it has proved. I begin to see why my father says you are formidable in court.'

CHAPTER SIXTEEN

'I WANT TO talk to you, Becca. Come into the book-room.'

Her father's voice jolted Becca out of a daydream. She laid aside the embroidery lying neglected on her lap and followed him out of the little parlour and into the book-room, reviewing her recent behaviour for faults that might draw such a serious-sounding summons from her father. She could think of none, but because she went in some awe of Nick, she was apprehensive of having done something to arouse his disapproval.

The mid-morning sun filled the long and lovely book-room with winter-pale light, eclipsing the firelight and allowing the eye to be drawn to the windows and to the dancing brilliance that was the sea at the lawn's end.

Nick sat down behind his desk and gestured to Becca to take a chair on the other side. She sat, feeling even more intimidated by this seeming formality.

Nick did not speak immediately. He picked up a pencil and sat tapping it abstractedly on the desk-top until Becca's nerves were drawn tight. Then with a sigh and a frowning look, he said almost irritably, 'You've had one proposal, so you must have realized you've reached marriageable age. Have you any thoughts to offer on the subject?'

The question was so unexpected that for a moment or two Becca could not think how to answer it, but then, making an effort she said, 'I did not like Justin Prescott enough to marry him.'

'That much I had gathered from the fact that you refused his offer,' Nick said drily. 'Lately, it seems to me, you have been in Lord Osmond's company with increasing frequency: I must suppose you like *him*.'

'Oh, yes. I find him very pleasant.'

'Pleasant enough to marry?'

'Marry! No. I have never thought of marrying Perry.'

'Most young girls in your situation would have done so. He's young, attractive, and has the advantage of one day elevating his wife to the rank of Countess of Ambershaw. The family is wealthy, with property in Devon, Wales and elsewhere. Ambershaws alone is handsome enough, Heaven knows. A match with the heir to an earldom must be considered brilliant by any young woman whose standing is no higher than yours.'

'Yes, but— But—' Becca floundered. 'I like Perry more than I ever liked Julian Prescott, but I don't want to marry him.'

'My dear, I know you had a very shocking experience when you were little more than a schoolgirl . . . has it made the idea of marriage distasteful to you? Are you thinking to remain single all your life?'

'I – no, I don't think so.'

'Then you should give some thought to the future. You are what – nineteen years old? Next April you will be twenty. Time is passing. Young ladies mostly marry between the ages of seventeen and twenty-two or three. It is something you should keep in mind. It is a sad thing if a girl misses her chances and is forced in the end to marry a man for whom she has little or no regard to escape being left a spinster for the rest of her life.' He paused to allow that dismal prospect to sink in before saying, 'Perry Osmond has shown you a lot of attention lately. Have you thought how you will answer him if you receive a proposal from him one of these days? If not, I think you should give it some thought. I am not suggesting for a moment that you should let worldly considerations of wealth and rank sway you, but they are not to be lightly disregarded when allied to a pleasant young man you say you like and one who has told his father he loves you. The earl was good enough to let me know he would have no objections to the the match.' He fidgeted with the pencil until it broke in two and then threw the pieces down in disgust. Frowning at his silent daughter, he said, 'It is held that females as a general rule, do not develop the stronger passions until after marriage. I am not convinced it is entirely true, but I think you should consider how well you like Lord Osmond. Lord Ambershaw's willingness to accept you as his son's wife honours you. Honours us all. We are not nobility.'

'I have—' She sat speechless, staring at him beseechingly until she found the courage to say in a voice little above a whisper, 'I – I have always thought I would marry Timothy.'

'Timothy! Has he given you any reason to suppose that he has marriage to you in mind?'

'No.' She lapsed into silence again before saying unhappily, 'Not since— No.' And then, a little waspishly, added, 'I rarely see him these days and when I do, Lady Helena always seems to be on hand to claim his attention.'

Somewhere between amusement and exasperation, Nick said, 'I should be more than a little surprised if Timothy had any thought of marrying you after the way you have treated him. He is a man of some importance these days – or, at least, well on the way to being so. He is far from being a fool and you have given him a poor return for his chivalrous behaviour towards you. And then to strike him as you did! For no reason, or for none that you have ever been able to explain. I think you will do well to put all hope of marrying him far out of mind. Sensible men look for peace and harmony in their homes when they marry. The choice for Timothy has widened considerably, while you, my dear, I am sorry to say, have shown yourself to him in the worst possible light. Not to mince words, you have shown yourself as ungrateful, ungracious and unladylike. Not the wife for a rising man. There have been times when I have been ashamed of you. Lady Helena, I imagine, provides a contrast that can only accentuate the difference.'

To hear her father put her worst fears into plain words, slew what small hope Becca had been able to cling to that one day everything would come right and Timothy would turn to her. She sat with bent head, hugging her misery.

Nick, too, seemed unable to think of anything more to say, but stirred himself presently to end, 'That's all for now, my dear. I just wished to warn you that Lord Osmond has marriage in mind and to urge you to think ahead a little and not just drift along as you seem inclined to do. One day this house will pass to your brother Stephen, and you might not find things altogether to your liking if he marries and his wife and you find you cannot live in accord. Nor, I think, would you care to have your presence in their home merely tolerated, any more than I think you would care to live the greater part of your life on the margin of others. Now go and think about what I have said. Don't let all your chances slip by you. I am not saying you *should* marry Perry Osmond, though I think you could do worse.'

'Yes, Papa,' she said meekly, though feeling far from meek. Her mind in turmoil, she gathered herself together sufficiently to leave the room before more could be said.

Seeking the privacy of her room, she sat on her bed and thought of the perversity of Fortune that sent her two titled men who wished to many her and withheld the one untitled man she wanted. From an early age, when she had first learned that men and women married and set up home together there had been lodged at the back of her mind, accepted without conscious recognition, the belief that eventually she and Timothy would marry. That had been long before she had learned that children did not just happen along at some time because of the marriage ceremony. She had Edward Jordan to thank for opening her eyes to a number of such facts as well as for being the cause of the errors she had fallen into afterwards. It was what Jordan had done that had robbed her of Timothy's love, she was sure, and though he had been prepared to marry her to rescue her from her predicament, when it had become unnecessary it seemed he had been glad to withdraw from the situation. And whenever she had tried to improve the way things were between them, she had only succeeded in making them worse; always lost her way between resentment, anxiety and longing. And now her papa had confirmed her unhappy fears that things would never be as she wanted them between Timothy and herself. He had also pointed out that her choices would narrow to the point of disappearing with the passing of a few short years and common sense required her to take stock of what her present choices were.

If she did not marry Perry, who *would* she marry?

CHAPTER SEVENTEEN

TIMOTHY READ THE scribbled message a fourth time: it made no more sense than his first reading had done. It had lain among the rest of his mail though it had not come through the post; a rough piece of paper, folded once, on which was a single line written in schoolboy's script.

Meet me tonight at The Dancing Bear. 8 of the clock. (And, as a signature) *An old Acquaintance.*

Why the anonymity? And why at The Dancing Bear? He knew it only by reputation as an ancient tavern on the outskirts of the city, ill thought of by anyone with the least pretension to respectability. He understood it to have fallen into disuse since the death of the last landlord. The only explanation of the note he could think of was that it came from someone down on his luck who needed a hand-out and wanted to be sure there would be no witness who could recognize him when he received it, but someone who did not claim friendship, merely acquaintance. He could think of no one fitting those circumstances who would be likely to choose to appeal to him for help.

He thought he had decided not to go, but at the last minute found his curiosity was greater than his caution and set out on foot to keep the appointment.

The Dancing Bear showed its rural past in its cob-cottage style, its proportions and the nearby remains of what looked like an old pig-pen. A small, decrepit barn was attached to the main building and the whole stood on a littered earth patch bare of any growth. Even the usual coarse weeds appeared to have made little or no attempt to invest this drear patch of soil.

There was just one dim light showing in one of the windows, but the door opened to Timothy's touch and he walked into what appeared to be the tap-room. What light there was, was provided by a single, smoky oil-lamp hanging above the bar. The only occupant was an elderly man he took to be the tapster who peered through the murky gloom at him as though a customer was the last thing he expected to see. A withered gnome of a man, he looked as if he lived in his clothes day and night and was unacquainted with the uses of water.

'Ale?' Timothy said, as an amused question when the tapster made no enquiry as to his wishes. 'You sell it, I imagine?'

For answer the old man fumbled out a tankard from a dusty-looking shelf, gave Timothy one more uncertain look, shook his head at whatever conclusion he reached, and turned to one of two barrels standing on trestles against the wall.

Taking the filled tankard from him, Timothy set it down on a scarred and stained table, and seated himself on the comfortless bench hugging the hearth where a few logs made a sulky pretence of producing heat. Time passed. No other customers ventured in. The tapster stared at the solitary patron of the house, scratched among his unlovely clothing until, as though forced into unaccustomed speech, he asked with a glance at the cloudy and still untouched ale, 'You waiting for someone?' And then belatedly, as though the word was foreign to him, added, 'sir.'

'Yes. An acquaintance,' Timothy told him, bored and irritated.

'Oh, *him*!' A spark of life briefly animated the tapster's face. 'Should have said. He'll likely be in the barn. It's where—' He left that, said, 'Come through the back. I'll show you the quick way.'

He led the way through a door at the back of the taproom into an even more dimly lit, low-ceilinged passage pervaded by a damp animal smell. Reaching a right-hand door near its end, he opened it to show it gave directly into the barn. As soon as Timothy stepped through, the tapster pulled the door to as though anxious to disclaim any curiosity in what lay beyond it.

With four lanterns hanging from low cross-beams, the barn was well lit compared with what might be thought the business quarters of the inn. As his gaze took in the four men already in the barn, the thought entered Timothy's mind that he had walked into a trap. But the expressions on the faces turned to him told him that he was as much a surprise to them as they were to him. A trap had been set, but not for him. It was already sprung and the prey taken. Three of the men were strangers to him, but the size and the vivid blue gaze of the fourth had a lifelong familiarity.

Recognition was mutual. '*You*!' Josh spat out the word tight-packed with disgust.

Timothy made no response. Nothing had changed it seemed: Josh still expected no good of his youngest son. But that issue must wait. The first necessity was to understand the situation. That it was for Josh the trap had been set, seemed obvious from the fact that, with his hands bound behind him and his upper arms tied to his body, he was additionally tethered to a central post. A captive Samson, shorn of his strength but not blind. Two of his captors were obvious bully-boys: burly, dour of face and, Timothy suspected, dull of mind. All the better if they were.

The fourth man's dark eyes held a sharper intelligence: a man of fifty years and perhaps a little more, an inch or so above middle height and brawny but running to seed, self-indulgence showing in his fleshy body and high-colour. Josh's exclamation had snapped the man's attention back to him.

'You know him? Did you invite him? Who is he?' He fired the questions in rapid succession at his captive, shot another brief look at Timothy and returned his gaze to Josh. 'Related? There's no resemblance I can see. Nor does he look like any seaman I ever saw. I remember two sons as tow-headed as you once were. A nephew, maybe? No . . . I remember now! There were *three* sons.' Intuition combined with recollection to leap the gap. 'There was a little copper-haired brat snivelling behind the woman's skirts.' He laughed and turned back to Timothy. 'Never tell me you're the third son! Did he fail to make a seaman of you and leave you to make yourself into something resembling a gentleman? Mary, Mother of God! All the world's a circus!' He laughed. 'Well, young Ryland, if that's who you are, whatever chance or purpose brings you here, there had better be a drag-anchor put on you to hold you here a while.'

It was not the man's looks but his voice that woke a hazy memory from the distant past in Timothy . . . his home invaded by large men – or so they had looked to his then five-year-old eyes – in naval rig, and the largest of them a man whose voice had a different cadence from any to which he was accustomed; a cadence he recognized now as an Irish lilt.

'I'm here by invitation, though not, I suspect, any of his,' he said, nodding towards Josh. '*An old acquaintance*, so the note I received said. But you need no anchor for me. I promise I'll be harder to get rid of than to keep. I'm all eagerness to know what's going on. For a start, who are you?'

'A note from an old acquaintance, you say? I sent out three alike to be sure of netting the fish I wanted. I wonder which fool delivered one to you. Well, never mind that. You're wanting to know who I am . . . I, sir, am Patrick Shamus Kieran Johnston. You won't remember the name . . . it was too long ago to make an impression on the young tyke you were then. Twenty years ago and upward, it was. I came back to this country only a month ago and bought the palace you find me in. Talking with an old friend, I recalled there was a debt outstanding and no reason I should not collect on it.' He slid a dark, malevolent gaze towards Josh.

'A debt? *His*?' Timothy again nodded towards Josh. 'What kind of a debt?'

'When I was here before, he had two of his men flog me. I thought it was time to give him his own again.'

'Why was it done?'

Johnston laughed and looked sly. 'I thought his woman looked lonely, so I gave her a cuddle.'

'Did you!' Timothy had the opening he had been seeking and his voice suddenly thin and hostile, he said, 'That woman was my mother. Had I been big enough and of an age to understand, I'd have flogged you myself.'

He got what he wanted, Johnston's full, glittering-eyed attention. 'Do you say so? And you a guest under my roof! There's a brave boyo.'

Timothy shrugged. 'My mother is valued by her husband and her sons. Her worth is one of the few points on which we all manage to agree these days. She is not to be mauled by a' – his hesitation was long enough to suggest he had difficulty in finding a usable word, long enough to be insulting even though he finished ordinarily enough with – 'a man like yourself.'

Johnston was shrewd enough not only to recognize the insult, but that it was intentional. His dark gaze locked on Timothy, he rocked on his heels while he considered this unexpected introduction into his intended programme. Through set teeth he said, 'Is that so? Above my touch, you think, and maybe thinking yourself in like case. Someone should have taught you the value of caution, laddie.'

'It's been tried. But leaving that and my mother aside, we

come back to my father. I've no quarrel with you there.' He flung a mocking look at Josh. 'Go ahead and flog him if you're bent on it. I've no objection. In fact, I'd readily pay for a ring-side seat.' His cool gaze held Josh's for a moment and he smiled unkindly. 'There's just one thing—' He paused, returning his glinting gaze to the Irishman.

'Well?'

'Maybe you know it, maybe you don't. He's an old man, several years past sixty. Big as he is, these days he has a weak heart, though he'll never admit it. Six licks of a whip and you'll likely have a dead man on your hands. You'll need a ready means of getting rid of a large corpse. But if that's no trouble to you, go ahead. I'll not weep into his grave.'

Johnston swung a long speculative gaze back to Josh. 'A weak heart you say. . . . He hasn't the look of it.'

'That's often the way. But it's easy to prove.'

'And you'd be happy to watch?'

'Why not?'

Johnston's dark eyes gleamed attentively on him and the residual sharpness of a mind that once had not been dulled by being too frequently soused in alcohol, probed for the motive. 'You'd like to see him humbled?' he guessed.

'Again, why not?'

'He's still your father, boyo. Or doesn't that count in this benighted country?'

'As I said, I owe him.'

Something surfaced from Johnston's earlier years when other and better instincts moved him. He regarded Timothy with a sardonic eye and said wonderingly, 'I'm thinking Josh Ryland got some of his deserts in his third son. And of the two of you, devil take it if I'm not beginning to prefer the old man.'

'*Timothy*! *Don't do it*!' Josh said, his voice loud and harsh.

Their attention entirely given to one another, Timothy and Johnston might have been alone in the barn for all the notice they took of the interruption. With soft malevolence, Johnston said, 'And you with the gall to tell me to my face that you'd have flogged me if you could?' He laughed unpleasantly. 'Well now, my valiant young fellow, I will tell you what *I* can do. And will. I'll take your wish for the deed and let you stand in for both yourself and for your father. Unless you mean to claim that you, too, have a weak heart?'

Briefly, Timothy allowed a look of startled dismay to show. 'No. But— But—'

With rough strength, Josh's voice cut across his son's floundering. 'There's nothing wrong with my heart, Johnston. Your quarrel's with me. Send the boy off.'

Without looking at him, Johnston laid a theatrical hand on his breast. 'Ah, but it's wounded me, he has. And me mistaking him for a friend.' His glittering gaze kept a black malicious hold onTimothy. 'It seems your dadda has more feeling for you, than you have for him.'

'Don't be fooled. That's his pride speaking, not his feelings. He has two sons who think he stands at God's right hand. I suffered under the same delusion once, but no more. It's an image of himself he cherishes however. He thinks he can bear all. Put me in his place and he'll appear to himself and, he supposes, to others, as a lesser man. It's the way his mind works.'

'What your dadda thinks is no worry of mine, but I've no fancy for burying a corpse, large or otherwise, so I'll take no unneedful risk. You've talked yourself into a flogging and we'll hold to that. The damned cheek of you has brought me to think I'll get as much pleasure, if not more, out of basting you than the old man.' His tone had hardened as he spoke and with open contempt he said, 'In Ireland a man doesn't take pleasure in seeing his father beaten whatever he may have done. So it's your pa who gets the ringside seat and you that makes the show. And now that's settled we'll get down to business.' He turned to one of his two watching henchmen. 'Lenny, you and Walt can help the fine young gentleman out of his jacket and waistcoat like proper gentlemen's gentlemen and persuade him to remove his shirt. Then you can tether him to the rail of the old cart over there.'

'I told you, your quarrel's with me, Johnston. Leave the boy out of it,' Josh growled frustratedly, but again spoke to deaf ears. Johnston's malevolence had found a focus promising greater entertainment and Josh found himself relegated to the minor role of onlooker.

Lenny and Walt had already laid hands on Timothy. He made token resistance, but they were expert in what they did, and in brief time, Timothy found himself roughly divested of his upper garments and his wrists secured to the broken-down cart. It was as hard to believe in the reality of what was happening now as it had been that first time in his father's barn. With the hope that it was true, he told himself that what he had once endured, he could endure again.

The last knot tied, Lennie crossed back to Johnston and spoke a few words in a low tone that caused him to rise from the barrel on which he had seated himself and walk over to inspect Timothy's bare back. That done, he grunted a laugh. 'So we won't be the first to lay a whip on you, my boyo,' he said. 'And you past your boyhood when it was done, I'd say. Some colleen's angry dadda, maybe?'

'Ask my father. I told you I owed him.' Timothy's voice was a sullen snarl.

'You don't say! If it was disciplining you he was attempting, he left it late. For what misdeed was he so heavy handed?'

'None of my doing. Which is what he neglected to check.'

'So you think the punishment was undeserved and will be thinking now that history is being repeated.' He laughed again. 'It's a hard world and that's the truth.' He walked back to the barrel and nodded at Lenny. 'You first. The whip's in that corner. Amuse yourself until I say stop.' He reseated himself.

Lenny put his full weight into his first strike and opened skin from shoulder to waist. Timothy drew a long hissing breath – it was Josh who cried out.

Though there was little good left in Johnston, he did not lean to the extreme of cruelty and he said, 'Easy, Lennie, we're not aiming to flay him in the first five minutes. Leave something for Walt to work on.' He cast a purely curious glance at Josh. An idle hour had allowed time for memory time to revive an old grievance and the idea of revenge had been an impulse that rooted itself in a soil made fertile by envy: envy of a successful man with a handsome wife, three healthy sons and a happy home. With envy had come malice. The expression he glimpsed on Josh's face now was an unexpected dividend. The son might have no love for his father, but what the father felt for his son was otherwise. Thereafter, he divided his attention between the two.

If Lenny took notice of the instruction to moderate his strokes it made little appreciable difference to what Timothy experienced at his hands. He found himself fighting a harder battle than he had fought before. But his determination not to allow any sound to escape him had somehow merged with the idea that his silence was necessary not only in support of his own self-esteem, but in some unaccountable way, in support of Josh's too. He clung to that as to a lifeline though it took all his considerable willpower not to lose sight of it as time passed.

Walt was halfway through his contribution to Johnston's entertainment when Timothy found his mind lapsing first into disorientation and then into near stupor. A few minutes later he escaped into oblivion.

CHAPTER EIGHTEEN

TIMOTHY'S RETURN TO consciousness was prologued by the sound of his father's voice repeating his name and was followed by the gradual realization that he was lying prone on the earth floor of the barn, his face and hair running with the water that had been poured or thrown on him and that Josh, also free of ropes, was kneeling beside him.

'Turn and sit up so I can slip your shirt on,' Josh urged in a low voice, his weathered cheeks looking pinkly damp, as though he had shared some part of the deluge. 'We're leaving.'

It seemed to Timothy that so deep was his weariness it needed an immense effort to comply, but with his father's help it was done and Josh slid the linen up his arms and very gently on to his shoulders.

'Now stand up.'

That, thought Timothy, was beyond his power and he shook his head.

'Yes,' said Josh fiercely in the same undertone. 'On your feet, boy. Right now! Don't give the Irish bastard best.'

Some slumbering memory from his boyhood awoke. At an early age, he had learned from his brothers to respond immediately, as they did, to that commanding tone in his father's voice. It prodded him into giving his entire attention to the business of obeying the order and somehow he hauled himself upright.

'Good!' Josh approved. 'Now we walk out of this place and go to Mason Street to pick up the gig. It will not prove far if you don't think it so.'

Concentrating on putting one foot in front of the other, Timothy was only vaguely aware of walking past the sagging door of the barn and out into the yard. Josh let him have the appearance of walking unaided, but whenever it was necessary, he found a large, sustaining hand under his arm. Making no move to hinder their going, their captors stood like three sons of Belial watching them. He wondered hazily how long he had been unconscious and what had passed between Josh and Johnston to procure their release, but his weariness did not allow him to pursue it.

He had no more than a blurred impression of their walk to the stables in Mason Street, of waiting for the gig to be made ready and being half lifted into it by his father. Seated beside him, Josh gently draped the grey jacket of his suit over his shoulders and laid the waistcoat across his knees.

Driving out of the city the cold night air helped Timothy's head to clear, but did little for his back which felt as if it were on fire. Yet from time to time he found himself shivering uncontrollably. Josh glanced worriedly at him.

'Lean close,' he said. 'Get what warmth you can from me.'

He did as he was bidden and though he gained little physical relief from the contact, he found a peculiar comfort from the companionable closeness that lessened other discomforts. The relief for which he now most longed was to lie on his bed and let go of everything. Because of that it pierced his drowsy mind that they were taking a long time to reach that goal despite the cob's brisk pace. He looked about him and said, 'This isn't the way to my rooms.'

'No, son. Though it will take a while longer, you're going

home so your mother can do what's best for you, and there's going to be no argument about it,' Josh told him.

Timothy found something close to a laugh. 'Would I dare?'

'Oh, you'd dare all right. You were a contrarious brat from the day you were born and have only grown more so with your years. Don't think I didn't recognize what you were about back there in the barn.'

'Not at first sight.'

'True. Seeing you walk in a free man set me astray. After all, you had promised me no good not so long before. But I'm not such a fool as to not recognize what you were about when you began needling Johnston to draw his fire to yourself. I've learned, son Timothy. . . . So you'd pay to see me flogged, would you? And there was the Irishman offering to do it for nothing. So knowing my heart's no weaker than yours, why didn't you let him? As you said, you owed me.'

'And still do.'

Josh grunted obscurely. 'You're a devious and tricksy good-for-nothing, but I'll say this for you, lad, you put a lie across as cunningly as the Devil's own stand-in. I suppose they teach you how when they turn you into a lawyer.'

'Well, no. Not quite that.' He paused to gather strength and finished, 'Just how to get maximum flexibility out of the truth.'

Josh laughed, shook his head and fell into a ruminative silence while Timothy continued to shiver spasmodically, his mind still swimming in some limbo between daze and doze. After a while, his gaze fixed on the dimly starlit road ahead, as though speaking to himself, Josh said, 'You told me if I used the whip on you I'd regret it, and I have. One way and another, young Timothy, you've made me pay dearly for the mistake I made. Watching Johnston's bullies take his revenge out of your hide this evening was not the least part of it.'

Timothy opened his mouth to speak, but as though aware of it, Josh went on, 'No. I know that was not your intention. As I said, I knew you better, soon saw what you were about. I can tell you though, that every stripe they gave you found an echo in my own flesh.' He drew a deep breath. 'To know you were taking what was intended for me brought my pride as low as you said it would. But knowing it was what you had chosen to do despite what lies between us puffed me up again to bursting point. It gave me the greatest pleasure to tell Johnston afterwards that you had fooled him, giving him the truth in a way to make him think you were lying and implying lies when he thought he was getting the truth. He didn't like it and I didn't mean him to. But I had made sure the ropes were off me before I spoke.'

'You were still taking a risk.Three to one is long odds, even for you.'

'It was worth it. But I tell you this, Son . . . I'll make him regret what he did to you.'

A shaft of purely vengeful energy animated Timothy. 'Don't touch him! He's mine! Not for what he did to me – I invited it – but for threatening *you*!'

Josh glanced sideways at this son who so often managed to surprise him and when he turned away to give his attention to taking the gig into the track across Mariott land to Blackthorns there was a look of pride and deep content on his face.

Leaving his father to explain to Prue, Timothy made his stumbling way up the stairs, memory guiding him through the darkness to where he could lie face down on the bed that had once been his. Prue soon followed carrying a lighted lamp which she set down on the chest of drawers, left the room and returned in short time with a bowl of water, a wad of linen and a pot Timothy recognized from his boyhood as holding the virulent-looking green ointment that was his mother's homemade family cure-all. Having set these things down on the night table by the bed, she set about soaking his shirt to ease parting it from his lacerations. When, with gentle manoeuvring, the shirt had been removed, she stood for a moment looking down at her son's mistreated back. Blinking back tears, when she had command of her voice she managed to say lightly, 'There cannot be another man who finds trouble as easily as you do, Timothy Ryland.' More briskly, she added, 'Now hold still while I lay a cloth on your back. Be prepared. It's wet and it's cold, but it will take some of the heat out of your skin before I use my ointment on you.'

When the cloth was in place, she said softly, 'Why did you do it, Son? Physically, Josh could have stood the thrashing as well as you and maybe better.'

From some deep well of feeling, anger again speared up through his lassitude. 'With me there to watch! Do you think I would allow *anyone* – let alone that Irish nothing – do that to him?' Indignation fuelled a last burst of energy. 'I promise you, Mother, for as much as he *did* do, Johnston will pay. I'll see his squalid tavern closed. And if he's wise, he'll be on the first boat back to that emerald isle of his before *I* reach him. I may not be a match for my brothers, but *him* I can match!'

Prue peeled the cloth off his back, dunked it in the water, wrang it out and replaced it, before saying softly, 'Against all appearances, you, my son, are a firebrand! Now, for my own particular comfort, tell me that everything between you and Josh is as it should be.'

'Yes. This evening – things changed. Seeing Josh helpless roused me to fury. Remembering my own behaviour on one occasion, I saw myself on a par with Johnston . . . saw myself as contemptible. I doubt you know this and I am ashamed to remember it. When he was still a sick man, still unable to leave his bed, you asked me to ease his worry. When I went up to him, he tried to say something about what had happened between us . . . tried, I knew, to express regret. I, to my shame, threw it back in his face. I don't suppose he told you?'

Prue shook her head.

'He shames me. I should take lessons in generosity from him! He – and now you – have good reason to think poorly of me.'

'For your comfort, I'll tell you, Josh shed tears for you this evening. Josh who never lets the world see his own wounds, wept to see what was done to you. He says it was brutal and not a squeak out of you from start to finish. He's both proud and humble. Because it was done for him. It's time you realized he needs your affection as much as you need his. I told you a while ago,Timothy, Josh is only human. As are we all. . . .'

Timothy turned his face deeper into the pillow, muffling his next words in its feathers. 'He never lost my affection, whatever I might have said. If I have his, it's more than I deserve. But I have needed to know it.'

Whatever passed privately between the Earl of Ambershaw and his son regarding Miss Mariott had made no difference to the frequency with which Perry sought that young lady's company. Nor did it make any detectable difference to the manner in which he approached her.

On this blustery December day, Perry, Lady Helena and Rebecca sat close together, their heads, one tawny and one black, bent over a sketchbook of views drawn by Helena and her mother while they were in Devon.

Timothy had sent word that he was unable to join them and having been told something of Helena's disappointed hopes, Perry suspected that his stated inability might be diplomatic. He was missed. Not only for Helena's sake but for his own. A trio did not balance as comfortably as their usual foursome and Perry decided he must make a bolder approach to courtship and find a way to have Miss Mariott to himself For a time he sat watching the play of firelight on his beloved's shining black coronet of hair and the pale, beautiful face under it and was lost in dreams. He awoke from these, suddenly, to say, 'Helena, have you yet shown Miss Mariott the house? If not, the gallery might interest her and the tower room.'

Helena, like a good sister, picked up the prompt and suggested that the omission be rectified immediately. Together they made a tour of the principal rooms on the first floor and Rebecca duly admired the painted ceilings, the decorated over-door panels and the magnificent fireplaces in two of the rooms.

When they reached the gallery on the next floor, Helena made a fluttering excuse about needing to speak to her mother and left Perry to name and explain the many portraits and other paintings to Rebecca.

Stopping before a full-length portrait of a young man, Becca said in slightly questioning tone, 'You?'

'No. My father. Thirty years ago.'

'You are remarkably alike, but I *sense* a difference more than I see it. The clothes are not so different: men's country clothes do not seem to change as rapidly as others. There is something else, though – a look. I think for all your love of funning, you have a less flexible nature than he has.'

'A judgement! Do not let it weigh against me, Miss Mariott, I beg.'

A little flustered, she said, 'Oh, no, indeed! Not a judgement. I do not mean to criticize. It was nothing more than a passing opinion that could be changed by many things.' She gave him a shy, uncertain smile. 'Even by nothing more than a change of light here in the gallery.'

Perry smiled back at her, thinking how delightful she looked when confusion brought colour into her cheeks.

They moved on and stopped again before another full-length portait of a young woman. 'My mother,' Perry said.

'Oh, how pretty she is!' Rebecca said, in genuine admiration.

'Many have said so. And I know my father thinks so still, though they have been so long married. Helena considers it very unfair that she more resembles Grandmama, Father's mother, than our mama.'

'But Helena is good-looking, too. Timothy says she is handsome.'

'Yes, so she is,' he agreed, adding with slow thoughtfulness, 'It is a pity it does not draw him into wanting to marry her. I feel free to say that because I do not think it is news to you that *she* is more than a little fond of him.'

'No. I rather thought it was so.'

'Well, her hopes are all at an end. He has let her know he has no thoughts in that direction. I am sorry for it because I am fond of my sister and regard Timothy as my friend. I would have welcomed a match between them.' He paused a moment, then said a little hesitantly, 'I should not pry, but I am daring to do so and ask if he has said anything of this to you? Do not answer if you do not care to. I am not asking you to break a confidence.'

She dared not meet his gaze for fear he should see reflected in her face the joy and relief she felt at what he had told her. It might be unworthy of her, but to know that Timothy remained free and uncommitted lifted her heart. It was still possible that he might turn to her, forgive her. . . .

Without looking at him, she said, 'No. He has said nothing to me. I have seen nothing of him lately. I believe him to have been unwell and have heard that he returned to his home and his mother's care for a short time. A bad chill . . . something of that nature, I was told.' She closed the subject by directing her gaze to the portraits again and said, 'Most of the ladies I see here are very beautiful.'

'Some more by courtesy of the artist than in truth, perhaps.' He gave her a penetrating look, said quietly, 'I should like to see a portrait of you hanging among the rest.'

'Oh!' She looked astonished. 'But that's impossible. They are family portraits. I should be out of place.'

'It is possible that you might not be,' he said gently.

For a moment she did not see what he meant – and then,

suddenly, she did. Colour flooded up into her cheeks and turning from him, she walked a few hurried paces further on. It was not quite flight but came close to it.

Perry sighed. It was clearly too soon to make obvious overtures. Hard as it was, he must try for patience.

There were no towers in Ambershaws, but from the gallery a stairway and a passage or two took them into the west wing and brought them to the so-called tower-room. It was built into an angle of the roof and was approached by a few twisting steps hidden behind panelling and known only to the initiated. The room was small, the window that gave it light was built between the rafters but set low so that it gave a view over the flat countryside lying south of the house and its grounds and towards the sea. This last was a shining expanse on fine days but was absorbed into what could be seen of the sky when the weather was grey. Furniture was minimal: a rug, a small writing-table, a chair, a shelf of books, a truckle bed. There was no air of mystery about it; no hint of a wounded cavalier or a hunted priest ever having been hidden in it. Nor were there any cobwebs or dust; someone kept it clean. It was all very commonplace.

'This,' said Perry 'is the punishment room for misbehaving children. A place of isolation. If, when we were young, Helena or I were thought to be unfit for civilized company through a failure of expected courtesy, or because of our unseemly appearance, we were banished to this room to reflect on our shortcomings. Discourtesy of any sort, to anyone, ranked high in my father's calendar of crime, and though if you have not experienced it, you might not think it a very severe punishment, it is surprising how deep an impression a few hours cut off from the rest of the household can make on a child. No sounds from the rest of the house penetrate this far and the burden of guilt weighs heavy in the silence. All the books are *very* improving and meals were prison fare of sugarless porridge, bread and water.' He laughed, remembering. 'Cook sometimes hid sugar *under* the porridge instead putting it on top. She took a risk, bless her, and she would have suffered for her kindness if it had become known, even if only from stern words. For her sake as well as our own, Helena and I learnt to mind our manners at an early age.'

Nothing more could be made of the room and they turned to go. Passing back through the gallery, Perry, attempting some gain from the tour, said, 'Timothy and Helena came to first names some time ago, but for some reason you and I have remained on formal terms. I still address you as Miss Mariott because you have never invited me to do otherwise and you call me nothing at all except a very occasional "Lord Osmond". Do you not think we have been long enough acquainted to come to Perry and Rebecca?'

'I – I think of you as Perry,' Rebecca said, surprising and gratifying him.

'Then will you not now use it and allow me the privilege of calling you Rebecca?'

'Of course. My parents and Timothy often call me Becca.'

He slanted a smile at her. 'I must not encroach on the prerogative Timothy's longer acquaintance gives him. Or not yet'

'Oh, he would not mind,' said Rebecca erroneously.

They came back to the room they had been sitting in then and shortly after, Helena returned, too, with a slightly flurried apology for her delay. The quirky look her brother gave her told her he had gained something from the interlude.

And so he had, he told himself Small as it was, it *was* an advance.

CHAPTER NINETEEN

IN THE WEEK before Christmas, The Hampshire Chronicle, one of the two local papers serving Chichester, carried a short item of news on page three that raised little interest in the general public, but was of particular interest to the Ryland family. It told of forced entry by members of the local constabulary into the premises of an old and half-ruined tavern on the outskirts of the city where several items of value recently stolen from local private houses were found. Named The Dancing Bear, the tavern was deserted and signs of a hasty departure were to be seen everywhere. The place had changed hands a number of times in the past thirty years, the most recent owner being an Irishman, named Johnston, who was thought to have since fled back to his own country. Johnston was reported to have had an encounter the previous day with a well-dressed younger man, unknown in the locality. Mr Wilfred Fowler, who had been employed as tapster at The Dancing Bear for more than twenty years under three different landlords, said he had seen this young man only once before and that about five or six days prior to the event. On the more recent occasion, the stranger had exchanged words with the new landlord. The exchange appeared to be acrimonious and had led Johnston to attack the younger man, from which attack the Irishman had emerged very much the loser. Mr Fowler had witnessed the quarrel that had preceded the attack, but was unable to say what it was about or whether it was in any way connected with Johnston's hasty departure. Mr Fowler, did not live on the premises and so could not say at what hour the tavern was abandoned, or if Johnston received warning from some source that the police were interested in him.

Early on Christmas Day Timothy rode out to Blackthorns. The door was opened to him by Josh. They had not met since Timothy had returned to his rooms four days after Josh had brought him home from The Dancing Bear. For the space of half a minute they stood regarding each other, slow smiles dawning on the faces of both. Their minds better attuned, a new confidence had come into being between them.

Timothy broke the silence. 'I am here more than willingly, Father. Are you willing that I should come in?'

'What need to ask! Come in, boy. Come in.' Josh hauled him across the doorstep and relieved him of some of the parcels he was carrying.

Taking advantage of this favourable moment, Timothy asked, 'Why do you still call me "boy"? At twenty-six, I feel I'm a bit old for the label.'

Josh stood still, looking surprised. 'I've never thought about it.' His smile widened to a grin. 'But now that I do, do you know, I believe it helps me to feel younger. You must have heard at some time that between Andy and Giles your mother lost two babies, both girls. There were four barren years after that before she gave me another little one. You. It made me feel good to have a young sprig about the place again. But you were the last. I think that without realizing it I have been holding on to the idea of still having a youngling around. Does it bother you?'

'It did, but not any more. Call me what you like. You'll probably be using some more opprobrious term before long.'

'If you use break-teeth words like that, I probably shall.'

At that moment, Prue surged out of the kitchen on a billow of rich, Christmassy odours and Timothy was engulfed in her greeting. 'We shall have you to ourselves until about four o'clock,' she exulted. 'The others will all arrive then and with five youngsters in the house, we shall be lucky to hear ourselves think. Especially when they see the tree. They have their own, of course. Wherever the idea for a decorated tree came from, it's a good one and has really caught on. If those parcels contain presents put them under the tree with the rest. The children are spoiled beyond belief with the number of gifts they are given. The days of one longed-for present from one's parents at Christmas and perhaps a half-sovereign from Grandpa if one was lucky, are slipping out of memory.'

It was a warm and comfortable homecoming and after the traditional dinner of goose and plum pudding, they were sitting peacefully by the living-room fire awaiting the arrival of the rest of the family, when Josh said, 'I imagine you were the well-dressed stranger with whom our friend Johnston of The Dancing Bear had an unfortunate encounter. *The Chronicle* made no great thing of it, giving it only about a score or so lines. Did you see it?'

'Yes. It was a fair enough piece of reporting. I went to see him with the intention of warning him to go back where he came from. I had revised my first vengeful intention and did not mean to lay my hands on him. The man's past fifty after all. But he clearly thought I was a soft city man and he came at me headlong, aiming to do as much damage as he could in the shortest time. So – so I stopped him.'

'With what amount of damage?'

'Oh, no more than a bloody nose and a black eye. Though I think I may have broken his nose. I could have done worse to him. Latin verbs and phrases are not all one learns at a public school. What they call the manly art of self-defence is also taught.'

Josh laughed softly. 'So it was in self-defence you broke his nose?'

'A little delayed. But I was out-numbered when we first met.'

They were given no opportunity to say more because Andy and Jill came in then with their three children, Phillip aged seven, more usually known as Pip; Pearl, aged five, and Mark aged two. Jill, blonde and in her easy way, a managing young matron, was another Prue in the making, and already rounding with her fourth pregnancy. When the immediate hubbub of their arrival had subsided and Prue had marshalled Jill and the children out of the living-room to remove their cold-weather wraps, Josh had been compelled to go with them, young Pearl having firmly attached him to herself as her escort. Andy and Timothy were left facing each other.

Andy wasted no time in grasping the nettle. 'Well, Father's told me that what you said to me about the division between you and him was the truth,' he said bluntly. 'The fault was his, so he claimed. Without questioning it, he accepted someone's word that you had behaved badly, and having got you in the barn, he flogged you. That's so unlike him, that whatever he believed you had done must have been pretty bad, but he didn't tell me what it was or who accused you. He said it was because it involved a secret that was neither his nor yours to tell. For that reason, I'll say no more about it, but I'm sorry to have added my doubt to his . . . to have let it come between us.' He held out his hand.

Taking it, Timothy said, 'It's forgotten. I did not blame you for standing by the old man.'

'He's told me since, what you did for him a week or two ago, too. That rates high with me, Timothy. The family owes you.'

'All the family owes me is my place in it. And it's all I want.'

'You have that, little brother, without doubt. But Giles never likes finding himself in the wrong, as you know. If he gives you any trouble pass him over to me. I'll soon show him his place in the family,' Andy said with a grin.

Giles arrived a few minutes later with his wife, Mary, and their two girls, Susan and Charlotte, aged four and two. Mary was a pretty young woman, small and dark-haired, and still learning to cope with Giles's moods which led to a somewhat variable home atmosphere, but had Prue been asked she would have said that Mary's natural determination predicted her eventual ascendancy.

Some time passed before Giles and Timothy were alone together. Giles's approach was roundabout.

'So not only in the right, little brother, but the family hero into the bargain. Pretty standing for you, but where does that leave me?'

'Where you put yourself, Giles Ryland. Stuck on a roof-top and having to climb down.'

'All right All right. So I was misled into making a mistake. But you must admit it isn't like the old man to think far wrong of any of us. And then to take a whip to you – *you*, the brains of the family! But brains or not, lately fool enough to take a second beating! Or so he said. Haven't you learned how to dodge yet?' Whatever Giles's faults, under his touchy temper, he had the same strong family feeling as Andy. He sobered suddenly and said, 'It was a good cause, little brother. Your heart's in the right place. I'm glad to see you home.'

That from Giles might be considered a handsome apology, but no more could be said because their respite from the children was over, too. The three eldest came whooping back into the room, demanding permission to open any presents under the tree that were theirs.

'Oh, there are none for you. They are all for the grown-ups,' Prue teased, solemn-faced, coming in behind them.

There was an astonished silence for the space of half a minute and then Pip said politely and carefully, 'I'm sorry. We should not have asked.'

Mark, two years old and not yet under the restraint of courtesy, burst into tears. 'Pwesent . . . want my pwesent,' he bawled.

Timothy sat watching the pantomime with a smile.

'Time you found yourself a wife, Son,' said Josh, sitting down beside him.

'Can't afford one. What woman would want to live in those two rooms of mine and no kitchen?'

'Each of your brothers got the deeds of their house as a wedding present from Prue and me. We'll do no less by you. All you have to do is find a girl who'll put up with you.'

'No, Father. I want no expensive wedding present from you and Mother. I've cost you more than either Andy or Giles ever have – school, university and law training. And then the partnership. But by April next, I shall at least be able to pay *that* back!'

'Do you think I want it back?' Josh was indignant. 'And you're wrong about having cost me more than your brothers. What do you think I paid for Andy's sloop and Giles's yawl? There's no difference between those and your partnership and I'm not a poor man.'

'You soon will be if you continue giving at that rate! I'm only offering what I see as fair. I've never lived at home here while earning a salary and so contributing to the household as the others did before they married. And I've never been of use to you as a seaman.'

'Well never mind that. You keep your money and get yourself married a year or two the sooner. You have a bit of catching up to do in supplying us with grandchildren.'

'You cannot be hoping for more! The din made by the five here today is enough to lift the roof off?'

Josh swept that aside. 'Are we agreed?'

'No. But we won't quarrel about it. I'll meet you as near half-way as the pride I inherited from you will let me.'

'Be damned to your impudence!' Josh said, between pleasure and irritation.

All hope of further private conversation was ended at that point by their attention being demanded for the distribution and opening of presents.

The New Year's party was in full swing at Danesfield when Timothy arrived and the public rooms were crowded. He was warmly greeted by Nick and Elise and exchanged a cool handshake with Rebecca. With more guests arriving, he did not linger in the Mariotts' company but lost himself in the general crowd where he was found by Lady Helena who was there with Perry. The older Osmonds had thought it too soon after the loss of the earl's brother to appear at a large party, but had acquiesced in their son and daughter joining it provided they did not actually dance. Circumstances had combined with Helena's intention to keep a distance between herself and Timothy following the episode in the gazebo and they had met only twice since and both meetings had been brief. Her manner was warm, friendly, and quite free of self-consciousness, though there was occasional wistfulness in her glances when she thought him unaware.

Regarding himself as an accredited suitor for Becca's hand, Perry had made use of any occasion he could to be with her in what for him was an unusually busy period. Mostly they walked in the gardens at Ambershaws or Danesfield, but twice he drove out with her in the Ambershaws' light chaise with Nannibet as chaperon. Any advance he made in her regard, real or fancied, he reported to Timothy who gritted his teeth and gave him what encouragement he could.

Timothy was standing watching the dance in progress when

he glimpsed a face that teased his memory for a name. It refused to come and in the end he let it go, feeling it could have no special significance for him if it was so hard to recall. The Danesfield rooms were more than usually crowded and he did not see the man again until some time later. It was not the vague familiarity that caught and held his attention this time, but something about the man's purposefulness of movement, as though that movement depended on that of someone else. It did not take long for Timothy to realize he was following someone and seeking his quarry; he saw it was Becca. The door of memory opened: the man was Edward Jordan. Without hesitation, Timothy started in pursuit.

Becca reached and passed through a door into the hall, walking its length, seemingly unaware of being followed. Drawing level with the book-room, she turned into it and without once having looked round, closed the door behind her. The man dogging her footsteps followed, closing himself in with her.

Quickening his pace, Timothy was only seconds behind him, opening and closing the door with as careful quietness as Jordan and remaining for the moment at the deeply shadowed end of the room.

Becca was turning from lighting the lamp that stood on Nick's desk-table and started with surprise at seeing the man now close behind her. '*You!*' she exclaimed, shrinking away from him, her tone one of horror.

'Yes. Are you not pleased to see me? Have you thought of me since that delightful hour or so we spent together two years ago?' He reached out to lay a hand on her arm and she cried with increased repugnance, 'Don't touch me!'

'Now, now, don't be foolish! Why should we not spend another delightful time together, doing what we did before? Somewhere comfortable, like your bedroom, perhaps?'

Covering the distance down to them at speed, Timothy

grasped Jordan's shoulder and jerked him round to face him, saying in voice choked with long-nursed anger, 'I've waited all too long for this meeting, Jordan, but by God I'll deal with you now as you deserve!'

Astonished, Jordan stared. 'Who the devil are *you*?'

'At this moment I stand for Miss Mariott's family. What else you learn about me will be delivered like this.' He let loose a blow that snapped Jordan's jaws together and brought water into his eyes.

After a stunned moment, Jordan came back at him and was stopped by a second blow that sent him to the floor. He half rose on to one knee and rested there for a moment before completing the climb to his feet. Timothy waited. Enraged by this coolness, Jordan launched himself at him, swinging wildly, but making no connection with his objective before another blow sent him back to the floor.

Timothy had little memory of what he did after that. The coolness and science with which he had begun vanished in a release of the fiercest rage he had ever experienced. It was only when he became aware of a weight on his right arm and a voice calling his name from what seemed a distance, that he realized that Becca was clinging to him. Her face swam slowly into focus and he saw the desperate anxiety on it.

'Timothy, if you keep hitting him like that, you'll kill him! You must stop. *Please*!' she pleaded.

Almost with surprise, he looked at Jordan – bloodied, dishevelled, barely conscious. Drawing a hand down over his own face, he said slowly, almost wonderingly, 'I think that for a long time I have *wanted* to kill him.'

'Please, please, don't!'

He was still grasping the thick handful of clothing by which, without being aware of it, he had been holding the other man upright. Released, Jordan sank to his knees. Hauling him upright again, slowly and clearly Timothy told him, 'If ever you go anywhere near Miss Mariott again, I *will* kill you. I swear it. Do you understand?'

Jordan pulled himself together sufficiently to mumble through swollen lips something that could be taken for agreement.

'Never forget it.' Timothy turned the man round to face the door and gave him a small push. 'Now get out of here. Go to wherever you are staying. I'll convey your regrets and excuses to our hostess.'

Becca and he watched Jordan's stumbling exit before turning to look at one another. 'I'm sorry,' Timothy said. 'I should not have made you witness to that.'

'I was never more thankful in my life that you were here! I was terrified. But you were so – so wild!'

'Poor little Becca. I have a bad temper. It doesn't often surface. But some things – what he did to you – looses the tiger.'

'Timothy. . .' She stared at him, moistening her lips, gathering together her courage. 'Was it only *what* he did? Or was it because it was *me*?'

He gazed back at her, the lengthening moments increasingly charged with emotions too long held in check Now only the truth would do. He said slowly, 'That he should despoil any young girl, was bad enough, but that it should be *you*—' He shook his head and left the sentence unfinished.

Her heart in her eyes, she said simply, 'I love you so.'

Such a poignant depth of honesty could only be answered with equal honesty. 'As I do you,' he said and, reaching out, drew her into his arms. Bending his head, he put his lips to those lifted so willingly to his.

All the frustration endured by each for their separate reasons during the long months flowed into and were wiped away in those absorbed and passionate minutes, but eventually some sound drew Timothy's head up. Jordan had not closed the door into the room and framed in the opening stood Perry Osmond. Past Becca's unaware head he and Timothy stared at one another. Then Perry turned and walked away.

CHAPTER TWENTY

THE OSMONDS APPEARED to have left early, for Timothy saw nothing of either of them during the remainder of the evening. To some degree he was thankful for it. His thoughts were chaotic, defying inspiration. What could he say to Perry when he did see him? What explanation could possibly satisfy a young man as much in love as he knew him to be? He could see little hope of smoothing the forward path for any of them. He had felt it necessary to tell Becca that Perry had seen her in his arms, but found her unable to share the depth of his dismay.

'I have given him no right to think that he has a claim on me,' she said. 'nor has he asked for any. I have given him no special encouragement and if I have disappointed his hopes, I am sorry, but I do not not see that I am at fault, or that you are.'

But Timothy looked back through a foggy mixture of guilt and sympathy. *He* had misled Perry by assuring him that he, Timothy, had nothing but a brotherly interest in Rebecca and allowing him to think he had a clear road in courting her. He had seen it as giving Perry a fair chance and Becca an opportunity she deserved. It had been done with the best of intentions – with which the road to Hell was said to be paved. He could not be blamed for Perry having spun what he saw as progress out of hope and small nothings but he had let him go forward with no warning of any possible stumbling blocks.

How Perry would react to having seen the girl he loved and hoped to marry locked in a passionate embrace with a man he regarded as a friend, remained to be seen. A space of time before they met might allow some drop in the emotional level of the situation and give hope of reason prevailing.

Midnight came with all its handshaking and well-wishing. The finale of the evening's entertainment was a firework display, which began soon afterwards. This Becca and Timothy watched through a window of the drawing-room, their hands linked in the sheltering darkness of the position they had chosen. When they parted, it was quietly and soberly underlining the importance of the change in their relationship.

'Tomorrow, if I can, I'll speak to your father. If not then, the next day for certain,' Timothy told Rebecca. He pressed a final kiss on the hand he held and went to give his formal thanks and goodbyes to his host and hostess.

He was walking through the hall to the door of the house when a tap on his shoulder brought him round to face Perry Osmond. Thin-lipped and cold-eyed, his lordship said with a nod towards the door of the small parlour, 'A few words with you, if you please. In there.'

Timothy walked into the lamplit room indicated and turned to face Perry as he followed and closed the door.

His tone as ice-cold and contemptuous as his expression, Perry said, 'We do not need to discuss what this is about because we both know what it is. The best way of dealing with it is the old way, in my opinion. A meeting between us is to be preferred to a vulgar brawl. I trust you agree?'

'Perry, hear what I have to say first.'

'Not a word. And correctly, I am Lord Osmond. Only my friends call me Perry.'

'Listen. Only listen. Duelling is a capital offence, as I'm sure you know—'

'But still the most satisfactory means of redressing an intolerable offence. As I see it, the *only* means. Do you mean to hide behind the law and refuse to meet me?'

Timothy rose to the sneering contempt of the question. 'Damn you, no. But I should prefer a civilized discussion first.'

That was met with a small ugly sound of dismissal. 'A discussion! With a treacherous cur such as you? *No*! Were you looking forward to sharing my wife? Perhaps have already enjoyed her favours? Was she protecting you when she withdrew the charge of paternity she once made against you? Do not trouble to answer. I would not trust a word you say. I want nothing from you but your agreement to meet me. Do I have it?'

They were of equal height and stood eye to eye, two angry young men. Through his teeth, his voice hard and sibilant, Timothy said, 'Yes, if nothing else will do for you.'

'Nothing will. You've met Charles Ridell. He will act for me. Send your second to confer with him. That, I think, covers all that needs to be said between us.'

With a bitter smile and a mocking bow, Timothy said, 'As you say, my lord.'

The mockery passed Perry by; he nodded, swung round and walked to the door. There, however, he thought of one more thing he wished to say. He looked back. 'Since swords are passé, your choice must be pistols. Make no mistake, Ryland . . . I shall shoot to kill. I advise you to do the same.' He went out, closing the door behind him with a snap.

It took Timothy time and thought to solve the puzzle of whom to approach to act for him. Luck alone jogged him into remembering Harry Tomlin, a friend of his Winchester College days. Harry lived at Halnaker, a hamlet only a short distance outside Chichester. Their friendship had not gone deep enough to bridge the separation of a number of years and Timothy had forgotten his existence until his present need arose.

Renewing an acquaintance in order to make use of it was distasteful to him, but hamstrung by shortage of time and necessity, he gritted his teeth and called on Tomlin. He was lucky to find him at home and welcoming. Throwing himself on his erstwhile friend's mercy, Timothy explained his predicament. A large, easy-going young man, Harry's agreement was reluctant and wrung out of his good nature when told the limitations of Timothy's choice. He balked however when given the name of Timothy's opponent.

'You put a bullet in the Earl of Ambershaw's heir and without the smallest doubt we'll both have to fly the country immediately after. What the devil are you about?'

'Don't concern yourself I've no intention of putting a bullet in Perry.'

'Well, if you mean to delope, I know I've read somewhere that it's tantamount to admitting you're in the wrong. You might as well apologize and cut the risks.'

'He wouldn't accept an apology. He's burning to put a bullet in me.'

'So what are you going to do? Stand and wait for him to do it?'

'I suppose in a way that's what it amounts to, but I'm hoping that Perry will have cooled down. To tell the truth, Harry, I've never fired a pistol in my life.' He gave a wry laugh. 'If I tried, I could be dangerous. It might be *you* I shot.'

'You're mad. All I know of the duties of a second come from vague memories of things I've read of old duels. Hazy and incomplete. Wellington and Canning's meeting was among the last . . . ten or more years ago . . . did you ever hear about that? Canning deloped and Old Hookey missed his aim. What else I remember about duels is that seconds are required to try and reconcile the principals.' A tall, untidy young man, he was marching up and down the room in which they were as though eager to get to grips with his problems. 'I'm sure my father has an old book somewhere, something to do with the code of honour and duelling. I'll see if I can find it . . . have a word with the old man, maybe. He'll tell me the meeting should be called off but he won't meddle. What the devil did you and Osmond fall out about to bring things to such a pitch?'

'Sorry, Harry, I can't tell you that, but I can tell you Perry thinks himself deeply wronged. In a way he is, but not in the way he thinks. It's something of a muddle.'

'Well, it doesn't take a great brain to guess there's a female in it, so I'll ask no more questions. Is Osmond really after your blood, do you think?'

'He was when he challenged me. I'm hoping he'll have cooled down a little by now and be less vengeful. If he'd only let me explain. . . .'

'As I said earlier, you're mad. And I'm mad to aid and abet you. Don't worrry, though, I won't go back on my word.'

'I'm very conscious how deeply I am obliged to you, Harry. I really have no excuse beyond desperation for involving you. And please don't think that as unflattering as it sounds.'

'The reason I'm agreeing to do it is because you're desperate. And I have a wretched feeling it's not a good enough reason!'

At this early hour the fields on the eastern edge of the Ambershaw estate lay colourless under a sky high and remote and equally colourless. It was the second day of the New Year and though cold, gave promise of being dry and fine for January. Standing on the thin winter grass of the field chosen, Timothy thought with a curious sense of detachment that with little wind and flat, even light, it might be thought a good day for a duel. Facing the Downs as he was, there was a small stand of trees off to his right and a strengthening radiance behind them heralded the imminent arrival of the sun. There was no perceptible increase of warmth yet, but wisps of mist were already lifting from the hollows in the Downs. Timothy wondered if sunrise would cause problems with how the light fell: if so, the sooner the purpose that brought them here was disposed of the better.

He glanced to where a gig and two saddle-horses were stationed on the chalk track running past the field, the means by which he, Harry, and the surgeon Harry had persuaded to attend, had come. There was still room for whatever means of transport brought Perry and his second to the meeting. This was almost immediately made visible as a light travelling chaise came into view. Briskly driven, as it passed, Timothy saw that a corded trunk was strapped behind it: Perry, it appeared, was prepared for a journey immediately their business was done. The chaise turned neatly and was drawn to a halt facing the way it had come. Two men got out, spoke briefly to the groom who had leapt down from the driving seat to open the door, then turned and walked into the field.

Leaving Timothy to his lonely brooding, Harry and the surgeon had been standing some yards off making desultory conversation. With the arrival of the chaise, they had fallen into silence and turned to watch as the two men it had brought walked towards them. There was a brief consultation between them and then they separated The surgeon, a neatly dressed, grey-haired man, moved to a small distance from the rest, a flat leather case under one arm. There, he turned his back and fixed his gaze on the distant view.

Timothy watched these preliminaries as though they had little to do with him and seemed almost surprised to be approached by Harry Tomlin who, halting in front of him, opened the slim box he carried to reveal two sleek black pistols.

'Wake up, Timothy, for heaven's sake. Take one of the damned things,' Harry said in a tone of exasperation. 'And be careful. They're at half cock, loaded and have hair triggers.'

Gingerly, Timothy took one.

'Remember what else I told you. Hold it down at your side for the time being, but bring it up smartly when you turn and aim for the middle of your target.' He shook his head and said in a tone of exasperation, 'Don't be a fool and for God's sake let's have no heroics!' Nervously on edge now that the crisis hour had arrived, Harry scowled ferociously at Timothy. 'This is the most stupid thing I have ever consented to do,' he complained. 'Osmond really does mean business and Ridell tells me he's a skilled marksman. More and more, it looks to me like plain murder. No, not even murder – suicide!'

Timothy, awake at last, said, 'Never mind that. Just be sure and get yourself away quickly afterwards. If Perry leaves me . . . useless, don't wait about. I shall be the surgeon's responsibility then.' He smiled crookedly, 'As for the rest, you may be sure the earl's people will be on hand to see the field tidied up afterwards.'

'I wish you would take your situation more seriously. It isn't a game, though it all seems too Gothic to be real! And what I did not think to do was to make arrangements to get you out of the country at need. I should have done. Arrangements have been made for Osmond, of course. Being his father's heir, he felt duty-bound to tell Lord Ambershaw what was going forward and his lordship insisted on it. Osmond's been ordered to leave the country the minute the affair's over, however it ends. Osmond himself is so certain of the outcome he's already halfway to the coast in his mind, while you, Timothy Ryland— Oh, damn you! You'll need God and the Angel Gabriel on your side and I hope They're awake to the fact!'

'Lord Ambershaw's right, of course. Perry would be a fool to hang about waiting for trouble. You, too. Get away quickly, as I told you. You're a damn good fellow, Harry, to have supported me at all. Don't let yourself become entangled in any after-doings.'

Perry's second interrupted their colloquy. 'Is there a difficulty?'

'No,' Timothy said, before Harry could speak. 'We're ready.' Looking again at Harry. 'Go on, Harry. I'll remember what you said: you remember what I said.'

Pistol at his side, he walked towards Perry who stood cold-eyed and expressionless, waiting with seeming indifference to perform a small but necessary chore. For a moment, hazel gaze met green. There was no flicker of recognition in Perry's eyes; he and Timothy might never had been acquainted, let alone have known friendship.

Perry's second, Ridell, a slightly older man, with better knowledge than Tomlin of the conduct of affairs such as this, had taken control of the proceedings, and said, 'Stand back to back. When I say "walk", walk forward *eight* paces. I shall count them aloud. On the word eight, turn and fire. I shall give no futher command. Understood?'

The combatants agreed that it was. They turned away from each other, their shoulders touching for the briefest moment. Ridell began his count.

Timothy turned on the word *eight*. Simultaneously it seemed to him, three things happened: a small bird erupted from a nearby gorse bush, there was an explosion of sound and he felt a heavy blow somewhere in the region of his left shoulder. After that – nothing.

Perry cast one glance at the motionless figure on the ground, but was apparently too sure of the accuracy of his aim to need to confirm it by a closer look. Having shaken hands with Harry Tomlin and the surgeon, he walked with Ridell to the gate where the chaise waited. The groom already had the door open. Both men stepped into the vehicle, the door was closed and the chaise was driven away at a fast clip.

The surgeon, having hurried towards the motionless body lying face down on the grass, knelt down and gently turned it on to its back.

*

Elise Mariott was more than a little surprised to find herself visited in the early mid-morning by an obviously harassed young man; a stranger, who, having barely responded to her greeting, plunged into speech with, 'You don't know me, ma'am, but I was told by Timothy's landlord that you and your family are good friends of his. I'm speaking of Timothy Ryland.'

'Why, yes, we are,' Elise agreed with a smile.

'Thank God! I imagine you know where his people live. I have been getting more and more desperate to find someone who could tell me.'

'Yes, I can tell you that, but do sit down Mr – er—' She glanced at the card Sharman had brought to her, 'Mr Tomlin.'

'Yes, ma'am . . . Harry Tomlin. I live with my people at Halnaker – Hill House.' He sat down, but immediately sprang up again. 'I mustn't delay. Timothy's in a bad way and still bleeding. I must get another doctor to him. Too much time has been wasted already.

'*Bleeding*! *Another doctor*! Has he been in an accident?'

'No – yes, I mean. I must find his home . . . somewhere where he can be looked after. Not that there is much— He has parents in Elswick, I believe. Will they—?'

'Yes, of course they will. Where *is* Timothy?'

'Outside. In a cab. When I saw the two rooms where he lodges in Chichester and the old man and no woman to take responsibility, I knew it was no good leaving him there. And the surgeon we had with us would only take us as far as the cab rank. It has all taken so long and no one able to tell me anything except that his people live in Elswick, though I know when we were at Winchester together he said his people lived in France. And then by sheer luck I remembered the name of the house he often went to at holiday time . . . *Danesfield*. Here. I have got it right, haven't I?'

'Yes. But I can't say I'm beginning to understand any of this, but if Timothy is badly hurt I think I should take a look at him, before anything else.'

Harry trailed her out to the waiting cab and Elise forbore to ask any of the many questions pressing to be asked. The expression of the worried-looking cabbie standing beside his carriage lightened by one degree on seeing Elise. Putting two fingers to his forehead in salute, and a hasty, 'Missus!' as salutation, anxiety rushed him into further speech. 'I can see you're not old enough to be his ma, ma'am, but if you could do something for him— You'll need help if you wants to get him inside, but he looks like a goner to me.'

Looking into the cab through the open door at the ashen-faced figure sprawled along one of the black leather seats, Elise was horrified. She, too, thought Timothy looked like a 'goner' – if he were not already dead! Though not Timothy's mother, the several months of each of a number of years that he had spent in her care as a boy had given her a maternal affection for him and it was with profound relief she found the feeble beat of a pulse in a limp wrist. With her usual efficiency, she set about organizing what needed to be done.

'Though his home is no distance from here,' she told the anxious young man beside her, 'his mother might not be there . . . might be with either of her daughters-in-law . . . more time would be wasted and he might even have to be brought back here. I don't think he is up to such toing and froing. The attention of a doctor is his greatest need. He can be put to bed here and the necessary messages sent.'

Hardly waiting for Tomlin's more than willing agreement, she summoned enough help for a door to be taken from its hinges to be used as a stretcher and had Timothy gently and carefully transferred on to it. The hackney driver was paid his fee and drove away with evident thankfulness and a groom was despatched to summon the doctor and instructed to make clear to him the urgency of the need. As the improvised stretcher on which Timothy lay was carried into the house, Elise ushered

Harry back inside, saying, 'Come in and sit down. I must see Timothy into bed, but I will send someone to you with a drink, of which you look as though you stand in need.'

It was nearly half an hour before before she returned to him, by which time she was looking nearly as troubled as her visitor. Sitting down opposite him she said, 'You must have had a very worrying time, Mr Tomlin. I haven't disturbed the surgeon's dressing, only tightened the bandages, so I must rely on you to tell me the nature of Timothy's injury. Were you involved in the accident, and are you yourself unhurt? That is something I should have asked you earlier and I must ask you to forgive me for the omission.'

'I am quite unhurt, ma'am. You see—' He broke off seeing a pit opening before his feet if he attempted to tell her anything but the truth. He said awkwardly, 'It's a rather involved story, Mrs Mariott, and I don't know the whole of it. But I do know the authorities mustn't hear of it. You see it wasn't an accident as I first said, ma'am.'

'Not an accident! I was beginning to wonder. . . . However did Timothy come to be involved in anything— No, never mind that. Just tell me what happened.'

'He fought a duel.'

For a moment or two Elise stared at him in wordless astonishment, but then, pulling herself together, said, 'I thought that madness had been put an end to. But go on . . . with whom did he fight a duel?'

'Lord Osmond.'

'*Perry*! But *why*? They are the best of friends!'

'There appears to have been a serious quarrel, ma'am. What about, I don't know. Neither would discuss it, and though Lord Osmond's second and I attempted to bring about a reconciliation it wasn't possible. Osmond would neither withdraw his challenge nor accept an apology. Not that Timothy was willing to make one.'

In deep dismay, Elise wondered what could have happened between the two young men. 'Well, they are unlikely to have fought with swords in this day and age, so it must have been pistols. But I have never heard that Timothy ever handled firearms of any kind.'

'So he told me. When I said *fought* a duel, what I meant was a challenge was issued and accepted. If Osmond pressed the challenge on him, I don't suppose Timothy felt he had any choice but to accept without appearing a coward. On the field, he stood—' Harry swallowed hard. 'He stood and let Osmond fire at him. At least, that's what it looked like, though he had promised me he would make some attempt to fire his weapon. It might be that he was just slow. Which Osmond certainly was not. I think it was only the report of Osmond's pistol startling him that made Timothy tighten his finger on his own trigger. Since he was still holding the pistol down at his side, it fired into the ground.'

'And after? What did Perry do? Where were they?'

'They were in one of the Ambershaw fields. Perry did nothing. I mean he did not look to see if Timothy was dead, or wait for the surgeon to confirm it. Timothy had told me that Osmond had warned him he meant to shoot to kill and it was clear that he was sure enough of his aim not to feel any need to check that he had. I'm told he has a deadly accuracy with firearms. His father had ordered him to leave the country immediately after the duel whatever the outcome of the meeting and that is what he did.'

'And the earl did nothing to stop the duel! I just do not understand how men— And duelling is illegal— A capital offence, too! Well, what's the use of talking.' There were sounds beyond the door that opened into the hall. 'I think the doctor has arrived.' Elise stood up. 'Will you wait?'

'If you please.'

She nodded. 'Help yourself to more brandy. Let us hope Dr

Bartlett can give us a more favourable report than the surgeon gave you.' She went out of the room leaving Harry to the gloomy recollection of how little favourable that had been. The bullet had been dug out while Timothy still lay insensible where he had fallen. With a shudder, Harry recalled the single cry he had given at the crucial moment when pain had shafted through the merciful unconsciousness that had held him until then.

Never again, Harry vowed, would he do anything so foolish as he had in allowing himself to be persuaded to second someone in a duel.

CHAPTER TWENTY-ONE

HAVING EXAMINED THE patient, redressed and rebandaged his wound, Dr Bartlett faced the fact that he was unable to give the young man's well-wishers an optimistic forecast regarding his progress towards recovery. His private opinion was that recovery was unlikely. He had been attending the Mariotts since Dr Fenton had retired some thirteen years before and looking at Elise from under level black brows, he said, 'I feel sure I have no need to assure you of my discretion, ma'am, but I think it better that I ask no questions as to how our young friend came by his injury.'

Elise nodded agreement.

'He missed instant death by no more than a hair's breadth and I regret to have to tell you his life still hangs on nothing more substantial than a hair. The surgeon who removed the bullet did as he should. He was skilled and accurate, but I suspect the operation was performed on the field, in haste, and in far from ideal conditions. The young man has lost a great deal of blood, but with youth and good health on his side he could pull through. Some patients delight in surprising one by winning against all odds, but I cannot say other than I think it unlikely in this case. A few prayers sent heavenward might help. Miracles do happen. I'm sorry I cannot be more encouraging.' He closed his bag, picked it up and said, 'I must go now,

I have other patients waiting for me, but I will be back this evening, unless you send for me earlier.'

Elise accompanied him to the door then went into her drawing-room to give Mr Tomlin as hopeful a report as she could contrive without withholding the fact that Timothy's condition was serious. If Timothy died and news of the duel came out, Tomlin, too, might have to cross the Channel for a time.

The hackney cab having been dismissed, a horse to carry Harry home was produced and Elise told him that if he chose to house the animal for the night and return it the next day, she hoped she would have better news for him then.

As Harry rode away from Danesfield's gates, Prue came to the house by the field path. Elise met her in the hall and the two women embraced. 'I wasn't at home, I was with Jill and your man took a while to find me,' Prue said. 'He told me you wanted to see me urgently, but could give me no idea why. Is there trouble? Is it Becca?'

'No, my dear. It's Timothy. Bad news, I'm afraid. He's been hurt.'

'Hurt! How?'

'He fought a duel with Perry Osmond. What the quarrel was about my informant did not know.'

'Is he badly hurt?'

'Yes, I'm afraid so.'

Prue clutched her arm. 'Elise, you're not trying to break it to me gently that Timothy's dead?'

'No. Not—' She had nearly said, 'Not yet,' and hurriedly changed it to, 'Not dead, but he is in a bad way. The surgeon who attended him first, removed the pistol ball soon after he was shot, but he has lost a deal of blood. I had him put to bed here rather than have him jounced about more than he had been. Doctor Bartlett has attended to him and thinks as I do that it would be unwise to move him. You are welcome to come and nurse him as I am sure you know, and a room will be made ready for you at once. If Josh chooses to come, too, he will be equally welcome.'

Prue nodded her thanks but her thoughts were all for her son's condition. 'Where was Timothy hit?'

'In the shoulder. Just above the heart. The lung was grazed but no worse damage done to it.'

'Where is he?'

'Upstairs, in the room he always occupied when he came to us. The second door on the left.'

Prue was already climbing the stairs. Elise followed her up and into the room where Timothy lay. It was noon and the day had fulfilled its promise of being clear and bright. The curtains had not been drawn and the sharp wintry light showed Timothy lying still as a corpse and as white. Shocked, Prue thought he looked as though waiting to be coffined.

Standing beside the bed, she fought the desire to gather him protectively into her arms. A fatal embrace, she did not doubt. Her voice thick with emotion she said, 'You would not think with his intelligence that of the three boys he has been the one to give me most worry. At least it has been so over these last two years and more.' Gently she lifted the bedclothes, looked at Timothy's heavily bandaged left shoulder and covered him again. Unable to hold back her tears she turned to Elise and was folded in her comforting arms.

Rebecca came into the house from riding with her father. On her way to change out of her riding-dress, she saw Sharman in the hall and asked where her mother was, wanting to discover from her if there had been any message from Timothy during her absence. He had said he would seek a meeting with her father on the second day of the New Year but nothing had been heard from him yet and it was nearly midday. As she reached the gallery, one of the younger maids came out of a bedroom with a bundle of washing in her arms and Rebecca asked her, 'Do you know where my mother is, Jenny?'

'Yes, miss. She's in there.' The girl jerked her head back towards the room she had just left.

'Thank you.' Rebecca hurried past her through the open door.

As her daughter came into the room, Elise turned from the window before which she had been standing at gaze.

'Mama,' Rebecca said,as soon as she was across the threshold, 'have you had word from Timothy yet? He said he—'

'Hush!' Elise commanded hurriedly. 'Timothy is here.'

'Here! Where? Has Papa been told?'

'Will you please lower your voice? Timothy is very ill. The last thing he needs is for you to startle him.'

'Ill!' Only now did Rebecca turn from her mother to look at the bed and recognize its pallid occupant '*Timothy*!' The word was a muted cry. 'What has happened? What is the matter with him?'

Elise moved to take the girl by the arm. 'Come outside.' She guided her reluctant daughter out into the gallery. 'We'll go to your room since it's near.' They walked a little further to another door which she opened and they went in. Rebecca swung round at once. 'Mother, please tell me quickly . . . what is the matter with Timothy?'

'He has been shot. Early this morning.'

'How? Who by?'

'Lord Osmond. In a duel he appears to have forced on Timothy.'

Losing all colour, Rebecca clutched at the rail of the bed for support. '*Perry*! Oh, how could he!'

'Did you not know?'

'No. Of course not! Men never tell you about things like that in advance. How could Timothy be so foolish as to let himself be forced. . . . He *knows* Perry never misses what he aims at.

And Timothy— What does he know about guns? I have never seen him handle one ever.'

'So the young man who acted as his second said. But Timothy would not allow him to tell Perry.'

'Is he badly hurt?'

'Becca, I'm sorry, but I have to tell you that he is. Doctor Barlett was not very hopeful of his recovering from such a wound as he has.'

'Oh, Mama! Don't say so! Just when things seemed to be coming right. And I love him so much.'

'We will do all that we can for him, you may be sure.'

'Why is he here and not at his home? I thought his quarrel with his father was at an end.'

'Yes, it is. But Mr Tomlin, his second, only had his Chichester address and realizing there was no one there to care for him properly, brought him here because he recollected the name Danesfleld from when they were schoolfriends and thought we might be able to give him some help. When I saw how ill Timothy was I had him brought in and sent for Prue. She is going to nurse him here for as long as—' She left that hastily and finished, 'She has only gone home to set things in order there and fetch what she needs.'

'Will Prue let me help her? I'll do anything . . . sit up at night with him.' Rebecca turned a pleading face to her mother.

'We'll see. Not to begin with. You have no experience of nursing and Timothy will need great care. Nannibet and I will help Prue, but anything you *can* do, you shall.' She fixed a penetrating eye on her daughter. 'Do you know what Timothy and Perry quarrelled about?'

Rebecca flushed, then paled. Slowly she said, 'I don't *know*, but I suspect that . . . that it was because he saw Timothy kissing me. We had finally realized we could no longer deny what we felt for each other. Perry walked in on us. We had no chance to explain and Perry behaved as though he had rights

. . . as though we were engaged. At least that is how it seems to me. If it was so—' Her indignation rose. 'Mama, he has no rights! He has never mentioned marriage to me and I would *never* marry him. I love Timothy. I always have.'

'There have been occasions when I have thought you hated him.'

'You don't understand! He made me so angry when he kept pushing me towards Perry. As though I *must* be dazzled by the prospect of being Countess of Ambershaw one day. He's so noble-minded – and such a fool! He made me so unhappy. And now . . . now—' She burst into tears, sobbing through the hands she held to her face, 'He must live – he *must*! Oh Mama – make him live for my sake!'

The days that followed were dark with a desperate anxiety that slowly, almost imperceptibly, reshaped into desperate hope. Doctor Bartlett came every day as did Josh, though he would not stay to sleep or eat. For most of that time, Timothy, just alive, with little awareness of those who moved around him and totally unaware of their emotions, lay silent and still in the bed. Prue naturally bore the main burden of nursing her son, helped by Elise, Nannibet and even Becca in any way she was allowed. Becca's complaint was that she was allowed to do so little, her role being chiefly confined to sitting by Timothy's bedside to keep watch when claims of their households called Prue and her own mother away and Nannibet was resting or otherwise engaged. She lived like a shadow of herself in the house, quiet and undemanding, only her eyes, seeming to grow larger by the day, begged for an answer to the question she would not trouble her elders by asking, '*He is getting better, isn't he*?'

A little before the time she was expected, Rebecca entered the sick-room to allow Prue to go to her lunch one day and found her adjusting the ruckled undersheet. In doing this she had drawn the bedclothes down to Timothy's waist and to give the doctor ease of access to his patient's wound no attempt had been made to put Timothy into a nightshirt. Timothy lay on his right side to avoid putting pressure on his heavily bandaged left. For the first time Rebecca had a view of the scars on his back.

Eyes wide, she stared at Prue across the bed. 'Great Heavens! He has been dreadfully whipped! Whoever could have beaten him so! Josh would never— Surely his school did not beat boys so badly?'

Prue, worn down by worry for her son and little sleep, answered bitterly and without thought, 'The first time, it was Josh. More recently and more brutally, he took a beating intended *for* his father. Someone was aiming to pay off an old grudge, but Timothy stepped in and redirected the man's malice to himself.'

'But why did Josh beat him? It's not like him.'

'It was when you claimed Timothy fathered the child you were carrying. Josh was so angry with him!'

'*Oh, Timothy*!' Rebecca stood stricken as she gazed down at him. '*That* was what caused the trouble between them, wasn't it? I knew something was being kept from me. How you all must have hated me!' She looked across at Prue imploringly. 'I didn't understand and I was desperate. Can you forgive me?'

Prue looked back at her. 'I did in the end, though it was bad at the time. But then I remembered how young you were and how frightened you must be with Elise away.' She shook her head. 'I shouldn't have told you, even now.'

'I'm glad you have. Not knowing led me into making mistakes.'

CHAPTER TWENTY-TWO

REBECCA WAS SITTING by the bed keeping the midday watch over Timothy when a visitor was shown into the room. It was in the dark days before the fever had broken and Timothy, though unaware of anyone who entered his room, lay in endless muttering dispute with his private demons.

The family was at lunch and the maid who knocked and opened the door into the bedroom was very young, new to her work and flustered by having been asked for Mr Ryland and Miss Mariott in the same breath. But she had chosen right in bringing the visitor here, she thought, relieved, for here were the two named together. 'Lady Helena Osmond, miss,' she said, and stepped back to allow the visitor to enter.

Rebecca came swiftly to her feet, the book on her lap sliding to the floor. Her action had the look of defence, as though she stood ready to repel any close approach her ladyship might make to the bed. Catching at control, with a slight inclination of her head, she said, 'Lady Helena.'

'Rebecca. . . .Miss Mariott. . . . I had to come. How is he?' Helena, too, was off balance. She dragged her anxious gaze from the haggard face of the man in the bed to look at the other girl. Unconsciously echoing the question that was always in the forefront of Rebecca's mind, she asked, 'He *will* recover, won't he?'

Coldly, Rebecca told her, 'We do not know. He has developed a fever and the doctor will not commit himself as to his future.'

She said nothing more and the silence that followed bristled with what might have been said. It was left to Helena to break it which she did suddenly as though the words could not be held back, 'I suppose you all – his friends, his family – hate Perry. Hate all of us.'

Unable to think of anything to say that was both remotely truthful and polite, Rebecca made no answer.

Anger flashed in Helena's expressive hazel eyes and she burst out resentfully, '*You* cannot think yourself without some share of the blame! Perry is flesh and blood like any other man. To walk in on a scene in which he found his intended wife locked in his friend's arms exchanging passionate kisses – how would you expect him to react other than he did?'

Stung into life, Rebecca flashed back, '*His intended wife*! You give me news, Lady Helena. Did Perry not think that I needed to be consulted in the matter?' Anger fiercer than Helena's sparked from Rebecca. 'But how could I be so unreasonable as to expect it! Perry is heir to an earldom. His title, his wealth, his condescension were, he must have supposed, quite sufficient to ensure my delighted acquiescence. It was sufficient for him to signify to the privileged few in his confidence that it was his *intention* to make me his wife. It was a pity he did not include me in that number.' She snatched a breath before to finish on a lower but no less intense note, 'If you are in communication with the gentleman you may tell him I despise him for having shot down what was in effect an unarmed man. Had he consulted me, I would have told him honestly that I would not marry him. I have loved Timothy since I was a child. He is, as he has always been, the centre of my universe. Whether he wants me or not, I am *his*. Nothing will ever change that.'

The silence that fell on them again was deeper and longer.

Helena recognized Rebecca's indignation as genuine and stood wondering if Perry could really have been so foolish as to let his love remain in ignorance of the depth of his feelings. In defence of her brother, with cold pride, she said at last, 'You do Perry an injustice. If he gave you no hint of what his hopes were, I am astonished. But if he did not make himself plain to you what held him back from speaking is modesty not arrogance. If his hopes outstripped the reality of the situation between you, he is to be pitied. He has been deep in love with you for months. I suspect the truth of the matter is that you were deaf and blind to the hints he gave you.'

Rebecca's mouth curled disdainfully. '*He is to be pitied* you say! But it is not *Perry* who lies in this bed close to death. We see the matter from very different points of view, Lady Helena. I think it is not possible for you to understand my feelings.'

A bitter little smile turned Lady Helena's mouth. 'I understand them better than you think.' Looking down at Timothy she said quietly, 'Some people draw love to themselves as naturally as the moon draws the tides. As he does. As you do. The rest of us make do with what we can get.' She turned from the bed towards the door. 'I came because— Well, never mind that. I will go. My presence is an embarrassment as much to me as to anyone in this house. I truly regret what happened. As do all my family.' Head high, every inch an earl's daughter, she went soft-footed from the room.

The days of dark concern slid at last into those of fearful hope as Timothy kept his frail hold on life and then slowly, inch by inch as it seemed, hauled himself back among the living if it was only to lie helplessly inert in his bed, even speech beyond the expense of effort. He could recall little of what had happened in the past weeks and his energy was insufficient to pursue the question of why he was here at Danesfield and not in his parents' home. He slept through many of the daylight hours and when awake, lay as though in a dream. He was in this state when he had a second visitor. Unlike Lady Helena who had reached him chiefly by accident, this one had to beg with a backing of many assurances, to be admitted to the sick-room. The hardest concession to win had been to visit Timothy alone. With patience and humility, neither of which came naturally to him, he won through and at last stood alone by the bed of the man who had once been his friend and whom he had been sure, for a time, that he had killed: killed coldly, deliberately and without compunction for despicable treachery.

Timothy appeared to be sleeping, but was not. Eyes closed, his thoughts were drifting aimlessly when a voice seemingly very near at hand said, '*Timothy. . . .*'

He knew the voice but knew too, that there was little probability of its owner being present in his room. Between the worlds of dream and reality where he so frequently drifted, he sometimes lost his way. This was one of those times, he thought.

'*Timothy!*' the voice repeated a little more insistently.

Half amused at his lack of faith in his own beliefs, he opened his eyes. Perry stood beside his bed.'

'*No!*' he repudiated the apparition. 'You're in France.' Rejecting evidence that left his mind unconvinced, he closed his eyes. Against the darkness he saw the oft recurring, unwelcome image of a grey field backed by misty downland. Perry stood at a small distance from him, a look of cold determination on his face, a pistol held at arm's length aimed unwaveringly at his heart.

But though his repudiation had been inaudible, Perry had read his lips and said now, 'I'm here. And looking at the biggest fool it has been my misfortune to meet, so far.'

The familiar voice impelled Timothy to attempt speech and even sparked awake a macabre sense of humour. 'Still alive . . .' he said, his voice hoarse and faint with disuse.

'Spoiling . . . your record.' His mind searched with exasperating slowness for what more he wanted to say. He found it at last. 'Are you here . . . to adjust the matter? You'll have to wait . . . if you want me . . . to stand.' Spoken thickly and clumsily, still it had been said.

'It's a temptation. Before . . . the way you stood . . . I supposed you had accepted execution. Given yourself up for dead. At sixteen paces, you *knew* I could not miss! What *I* hadn't counted on was God taking a hand. It was the bird that flew out of the gorse at the last moment that saved you. It could have shifted my aim no more than the scant shaving of a shadow, but it was enough.'

So it had been, but substituting pain, weakness and weeks of helplessness for instant death. Timothy's lips twisted. Gratitude, like many another offering made to God, was apt to be made with reservations.

The room was very still; the silence thick and heavy. Timothy sensed that a core of unappeased anger still burned in Perry. Perhaps his own gibe about adjusting the matter had not been so far out. He waited.

'I can outlive missing my shot,' Perry said at last, his voice hard and grudging. 'What I dislike is being laid open to the charge of shooting a sitting duck. I am certain you told me at sometime that you were a good shot. What the devil were you trying to prove, just standing there, making no attempt to fire? Not even to delope.'

'Couldn't . . . too slow. Never fired a gun before . . . Tomlin annoyed.'

'So I should think! So Helena wrote. I could not believe it. I thought no one could be so stupid.'

'Well. . . .' Timothy said.'

'And don't tell me you did not tell me you had no interest in Rebecca Mariott! One way and another you've made me look like the arch-fiend crossed with the village idiot.'

'Did it for the best . . . Nothing to offer Becca myself. . . *You* . . . very different matter. Thought she'd make. . . .splendid countess.'

'And you're supposed to be intelligent! You've wreaked havoc in my family. Helena is in the dumps because of you. And my father was first furious with me for proposing a duel that put his heir at risk. Later, when he learned I'd gone out against a man who had never fired a gun he wrote me a letter that cut my character into very small pieces. I am banished to the Continent until he gives me permission to return. So your first thought was correct – I am *not* here, even if you now think I am.'

Timothy laughed, winced and subsided.

Perry stood looking down at his drawn and pallid face for several moments more, his own expression carefully unrevealing. Finally, he said, 'I was told not to tire you, so it is time I left. It might speed your recovery to contemplate that honour probably dictates I should stand and allow you to take a shot at me when you are able,' Perry said. 'If you send me your cartel, I will accept it, but I advise some practice first.'

Timothy smiled and said nothing.

'You may well smile. The thought that makes me tremble is that given your taste for chivalry you might attempt to miss me if we do meet again in such a way. That might well put me in danger.' Briefly, he laid a hand on Timothy's undamaged shoulder. 'I wish you well, though Heaven knows why I should. Grudgingly, I even acknowledge your prior claim to Miss Mariott's affections while both applauding and deploring her taste in choosing you. But my fund of goodwill towards you, Timothy Ryland, is meagre, so do not put any further strain on it. I do not find it easy to forgive your misleading me. I am not a child in need of protection from the facts of life. So don't ask me to dance at your wedding. Unlike you, I have no natural inclination towards nobility and I won't do it.' He grunted something close to a laugh. 'But I am honestly thankful not to have your death on my conscience and by the time you have a son ready for christening I might have reached a sufficient state of grace to accept an invitation to be godfather. That's if you should be large-minded enough to think me eligible.'

He did not wait for Timothy to answer but turning, walked quickly out of the room.

CHAPTER TWENTY-THREE

PROPPED UP BY pillows, Timothy was listening to Rebecca read Disraeli's *Tancred* and watching her face through half-closed eyes. The maid, Jenny, sat by the fire, industriously hemming new pillowcases, an occupation much to be preferred to polishing brass fenders and doorknobs.

It was a typically grey February day with rain splattering the windows but wax candles had been lit for both reader and sewer. Already cheered by firelight, the gentle gold brought the pale-green walls of the room into richer life and glimmered on the bronze of the main curtains heightening the comparison Timothy made with his rooms in Chichester.

Coming on one of his occasional visits to the invalid, Nick nodded at the maid and said, 'You are expected below for the midday meal, Jenny, so off you go.'

'Thank you, sir.' Jenny folded her work neatly, laid it aside and went.

His hand on the back of Rebecca's chair, Nick looked down at the book she held. 'What am I interrupting?'

Glancing at the title page Rebecca showed him, he nodded recognition. 'I've read it. Well disguised ideology. He's a clever man.' He gave the chair a small shake. 'Give me your place. You, too, are expected below, young lady, so don't keep your mother waiting.'

When Rebecca was on her feet however, Timothy made a sudden decision. Now or never. No, not that, but *now* for fear that later something might prevent. He said, 'Rebecca', and when she looked at him, held out his right hand. Something in his expression must have warned her of the importance of this moment. She turned back to the bed and put her left hand into the one held out to her.

Nick watched this with faintly frowning curiosity.

'Mr Mariott . . . sir . . . I have something to ask you,' Timothy told him.

Nick's eyebrows lofted. 'That sounds very formal, Timothy.'

'Yes, sir. I am making a formal request for your permission to ask Rebecca to marry me as soon as I can leave this infernal bed.' If he had not outgrown blushing he would have blushed then for his lack of grace. 'I beg your pardon, sir. I was speaking of it as my own. I have been more than grateful for its comfort and for all the kindness you and Mrs Mariott have shown me, but I cannot help looking forward to the day when I am up and leading a normal life.'

'Is marrying Becca your idea of repaying our kindness?' It was said as a joke, but there was an edge to it.

'Good God, no, sir. How could you think it?'

'Easily, looking back over the past two years and remembering the devil's dance my daughter has led you. If it is not repayment you have in mind, then I have no hesitation in simply giving you a straightforward refusal.'

In the silence that followed, Timothy gathered his forces. His voice a little unsteady, he said, 'I thought it possible – probable even – that you would not like it. Might refuse. It cannot be the kind of marriage you hoped for her. Because of that, I have held back my hopes and wishes for a long time, but I love her very much and when, recently, she told me that she loves me, I—' He let that slide away from him, gave Rebecca a fleeting glance and deeply earnest, said, 'I would take the greatest care of her. Leave nothing undone to give her a life as near as possible to what she had always known. I cannot make myself out to be better than I am, because you know only too well all there is to know about me.'

'Good God, man, are you supposing I think you're not good enough! Your star's in the ascendant. You'll probably win a knighthood before you reach forty-five. What I recommend is that in the light of what happened to you through Rebecca in the recent past, you consider if she is the wife you need. The wife of a professional man should be be an asset, not an encumbrance.'

'Rebecca has never been that to me and no amount of considering will alter what I feel for her.'

'Will it not, Timothy? Think! You must have observed how ephemeral human emotions are. How little to be depended on they are. When you have met a few more young ladies, your view of the kind of wife you want may undergo significant change.'

'You may be right. But I have had close at hand examples of very enduring human attachments . . . that of my own parents and with respect, sir, that of yours and Mrs Mariott.'

'I cannot dispute your point. But there are no guarantees. And when there have been straws in the wind, a wise man . . . well, ask yourself if you are not hoping for too much from my little butterfly.' He turned a sharp look on his daughter. 'It would not surprise me to learn she has blackmailed you into this.'

'*Papa*!

'You wrong her, sir. Becca has done her best to keep her distance from me, thinking I could not love her after the disaster of her encounter with Edward Jordan. Equally as far astray in my thinking, I believed she could not fail to prefer Perry Osmond to myself. I thought, too, that she would make a splendid countess.'

'*Papa!*' Rebecca thrust in again, her tone demanding attention. 'You reminded me recently that soon I shall be twenty years old. Which means that the following year I shall be twenty-one. If Timothy will wait the fifteen months between, I shall marry him then, when I no longer need your permission.'

'Will you indeed!' Nick looked his surprise at this bold show of opposition from his daughter. It had sometimes puzzled him that he and Elise – the woman he had once named *the quiet rebel* – should have produced so tame a spirit as Rebecca sometimes seemed to him. There was no evidence of tameness in the glittering gaze locked on him now and it occurred to him that there might never before have been something she valued for which she needed to fight.

'Then I can only hope Timothy comes to his senses before then,' he said with deliberate abrasiveness, more than half expecting her defiance to collapse.

But Rebecca turned to Timothy and asked with a smile, 'Will you, Timothy?'

Timothy answered her only with pressure on her hand, his attention fixed on Nick.

'Sir,' he said 'if you will take into account that it has only been when Becca and I have been separated by misunderstanding that trouble has fallen on us, you may find what draws us together easier to understand. From the time you first took me into your home this day, even this hour, were, I think, predestined. She is necessary to me. Apart we draw the lightning – together I think we might conquer the world.'

He glanced back at Rebecca then as though for confirmation and the look they exchanged took Nick back across the years to a candlelit room in the nearby Sussex Oak when he had first said to Elise, *I love you*, and she had asked *Are you sure?* mocking his long unwillingness to risk putting himself in her power. On the faces of the two young people standing before him there was nothing to be seen but triumphant certainty. *As well attempt to hold back the tide!* he thought and sighed. They, in common with the rest of humanity must take their chance.

'Very well,' he said. 'I withdraw my refusal. Go and conquer your world together and pray God is on your side.'

They had forgotten him almost before he had finished speaking and, remembering the rapture of the dragon-hour of first commitment, he gave them one last look of smiling envy before turning to the leave the room. 'You have five minutes to celebrate your first victory,' he told them as he walked towards the door, 'then Rebecca, you will go down to your mother. Meanwhile, don't forget Timothy is still an invalid.' He went out, closing the door on them.

Looking up into Rebecca's luminously joyful face, Timothy said in a voice grown suddenly husky, 'I imagine we may think ourselves promised.'

She laughed tremulously. 'Oh I promised you to myself when I was six years old. It has just taken you a long time to accept the fact.' With a deep sigh of fulfilment, she sank to her knees beside the bed and laid her lips on his.